ALICE-MIRANDA
in Paris

JACQUELINE HARVEY

ALICE-MIRANDA
in Paris

RED FOX

ALICE-MIRANDA IN PARIS

A RED FOX BOOK 978 1 849 41860 7

Published in Great Britain by Red Fox,
an imprint of Random House Children's Publishers UK
A Random House Group Company

Originally published in Australia by Random House Australia in 2013

This edition published 2014

1 3 5 7 9 10 8 6 4 2

Text copyright © Jacqueline Harvey, 2013

The right of Jacqueline Harvey to be identified as the author of this work has been asserted in
accordance with the Copyright, Designs and Patents Act 1988.

The Random House Group Limited supports the Forest Stewardship Council® (FSC®), the
leading international forest-certification organisation. Our books carrying the FSC label are
printed on FSC®-certified paper. FSC is the only forest-certification scheme supported by the
leading environmental organisations, including Greenpeace. Our paper procurement
policy can be found at www.randomhouse.co.uk/environment.

MIX
Paper from
responsible sources
FSC® C016897

RANDOM HOUSE CHILDREN'S PUBLISHERS UK
61–63 Uxbridge Road, London W5 5SA

www.**randomhousechildrens**.co.uk
www.**totallyrandombooks**.co.uk
www.**randomhouse**.co.uk

Addresses for companies within The Random House Group Limited can be found at:
www.randomhouse.co.uk/offices.htm

THE RANDOM HOUSE GROUP Limited Reg. No. 954009

A CIP catalogue record for this book is available from the British Library.

Printed and bound in Great Britain by Great Britain
by CPI Group (UK) Ltd, Croydon, CR0 4YY

For Ian, who took me to Paris, and for Sandy,
without whom this journey might never have begun.

Glossary of French terms

anglais	English
atelier	artist's workshop
au contraire	on the contrary
bonjour	hello
Ça vous dérange?	Do you mind?
croque monsieur	a toasted ham and cheese sandwich
délicieux	delicious
désolé	sorry
Fil d'Or	golden thread
hôtel de ville	town hall
Île de la Cité	island in the middle of the river Seine
merci	thank you
mon amour	my love
Je m'appelle . . .	my name is . . .
Pas chinchilla! Vigogne, tu comprends?	Not chinchilla! Vicuña, you understand?
Nous avons été volés!	We have been robbed!
oui	yes
Pont d'Arcole	bridge across the Seine
Pont de l'Archevêché	bridge across the Seine (literally 'the Archibishop's bridge')
privé	private
Que faites-vous?	What are you doing?
Sacré bleu	An exclamation of surprise

Chapter 1

Christian Fontaine cradled his chin in his left hand and tapped his forefinger against his lip.

'It's breathtaking,' his assistant Adele sighed. 'I think it's the most beautiful gown you have ever created.'

Christian said nothing. He reached forward to stroke the buttercup-coloured silk of the dress's skirt. He hadn't used that colour for years. When Adele had suggested that it would be perfect for the final gown in the show, he'd agreed. Now, he didn't know if he could bring himself to include the gown, fabulous as it was. It was *her* colour. It always would be.

Christian turned and stared through the window across the rooftops of Paris. They seemed to go on for ever. He wondered where on earth she could possibly be.

Pain gripped his chest. He closed his eyes and tried to remember. Her laugh, her smile, the way she would call him *mon amour*. It was hard to believe how many years had passed. He could almost smell her perfume, the memory seemed so real. *Why did you do it?* He thought to himself. *Why, when I loved you so much?*

'What's wrong, monsieur?' said Adele. She had been worried about her boss for weeks. This gown seemed to have caused him more angst than anything else in the collection.

'Nothing is wrong, Adele. I am just . . . surprised.' He looked at her and smiled. Over the years, Christian had employed many assistants but Adele was by far his favourite, despite knowing almost nothing about fashion when she started. At the time, he'd wondered if she would last a week. She had confused bolts of fabric with metal bolts used for construction; it had not been a promising start. But she was a fast learner and she made him laugh, which no one else had managed in years.

'Surprised? Why?'

'I did not think I had the capacity for anything as lovely as this.' He stared at the gown once more.

Adele wondered what he was talking about. All of Christian's gowns were stunning.

'Do you have a pencil?' Christian asked. 'I seem to have misplaced mine.'

Adele fished around in her apron pocket. She found a pencil, along with the envelope she'd forgotten to pass on to him earlier. She held both items out in front of her.

'Oops,' she said, biting her lip.

'What is this?' Christian frowned at the fancy script that spelled out his name.

'An invitation to Madame Rochford's townhouse tomorrow evening. She's hosting a dinner party and everyone will be there.' Adele smiled at him expectantly.

Christian shook his head. 'Please telephone Madame Rochford and let her know that I am unable to attend. And send her something from the collection as a thank you for her kindness.'

Adele did nothing to hide her disappointment.

'But monsieur, Madame Rochford is so lovely. And so . . . single.'

'Yes, she is,' Christian replied. 'But I am far too busy.'

Adele sighed. 'You will never find love if you spend all your time here, monsieur.'

'Thank you for your concern, Adele,' Christian said sharply.

The young woman rolled her eyes. 'Don't blame me when you're old and lonely.' She glanced at the clock on the wall. 'Oh dear, is that the time? I must run some errands before I meet Jacques for lunch. He said he has a surprise for me.' Adele winked at her boss. 'Is there anything else you need?'

Christian shook his head. 'No, thank you, Adele. I'm going to cut the cape, but you can go.'

There was one piece left to finish the collection. It was the most expensive by far and Christian hadn't wanted to start it until the last of the gowns was done. Hand-dyed in the same buttercup shade as the gown, it would be a simple cape, made from the finest yarn in the world. He'd been warned that the fabric was so delicate it could be damaged when dyed, but he'd been willing to take the risk. He would work through the night to get it done – it wouldn't be the first time and surely wouldn't be the last either.

Christian was famed for the breadth of his talents. He not only designed but cut and sewed his creations, particularly the show-stopper gowns. He preferred to work alone on the fourth floor, while the seamstresses' sewing machines hummed like beehives on the floors below. It hadn't always been this way.

Adele gathered her handbag and a small pile of letters for the post.

'Are you nervous?' she asked. Adele would have been petrified. The bolt of fabric was worth more than her year's wages.

Christian shook his head again. 'I must treat this piece like any other.'

'Except that it's not, really,' Adele reminded him.

'Are you trying to make me anxious?' Christian scolded. 'Why don't you run along and get your jobs done.'

He walked towards the climate-controlled store-room and opened the door.

'Adele,' he called. 'Has anyone been in here today?'

His assistant scurried back across the warehouse floor and stood in the doorway.

'No, monsieur,' she replied.

Christian looked at the shelf.

'It's not here,' he said. 'And there are other bolts missing too.'

Adele's eyes widened. 'Perhaps someone has been tidying up?' she suggested hopefully as she scanned the immaculately kept shelves.

Christian Fontaine prided himself on having the neatest storeroom and workroom in the business. His staff knew that they moved things at their peril.

'Get everyone up here now,' he growled. 'If someone has moved that fabric, they will be moving too – straight to the unemployment line.'

Adele scampered away to round up the staff. Her mouth was dry and her heart was thumping.

Christian knew that the next few minutes were really just a formality. He'd been robbed and whoever had done it had known exactly where to look.

Chapter 2

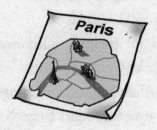

'Oh wow, look at that!' Jacinta exclaimed as she pointed at an impressive building in the distance. The limestone mansion glistened in the summer sunshine.

'It's the hôtel de ville,' Millie replied. She had been consulting her guidebook as the group marched along the northern side of the river Seine. 'But it's not a hotel. It's the mayor's office. Pretty fancy, hey?'

'I'll say. Paris is so beautiful,' said Jacinta, as the children passed yet another magnificent row of townhouses. 'It's no wonder they call it the City of Love.'

'I think they call it the City of Light, don't they?' Millie corrected her.

'Love, light, whatever. When I'm older I want to be proposed to under the Eiffel Tower.' Jacinta glanced back towards Lucas, who was dawdling along with Sep. 'Did you hear what I said?' she asked.

'What?' the boys replied in unison.

'The Eiffel Tower, my proposal?'

Sep and Lucas shrugged.

'Oh, forget it.' Jacinta rolled her eyes. 'You're such . . . boys!'

Millie and Alice-Miranda exchanged giggles.

A small group of students from Winchesterfield-Downsfordvale Academy for Proper Young Ladies and Fayle School for Boys made up the Winchester-Fayle Singers. The choir had formed in the months since the schools' very successful joint production of *Snow White and the Seven Dwarfs*. Led by Fayle's English and Drama teacher, Harold Lipp, and accompanied by Winchesterfield-Downsfordvale's Music teacher, Cornelius Trout, the group had quickly grown into an accomplished ensemble. Mr Lipp had been thrilled to receive an invitation to bring the group to perform in Paris during Fashion Week, when the world's best designers show their seasonal collections to the rest of the world. This year the organizers were keen to involve choral groups to give the festival a very different sort of flair. The Winchester-Fayle Singers hadn't been the organizers' first choice, but when another choir had pulled out at the last minute, Mr Lipp was offered the opportunity by his sister, who worked for the event.

So, twenty students and eight adults from the schools had arrived in Paris early that morning and been dropped in the centre of the city, from which point Miss Grimm had led them on a very long walk. Their bags were being delivered to the hotel, so they'd be there when the rooms were ready later in the afternoon. The choir had a week to explore the city and prepare for their series of performances.

Millie and Alice-Miranda walked ahead of the other girls, quickly catching up to the headmistress.

'Excuse me, Miss Grimm,' said Alice-Miranda. 'May I ask where we're going now?'

'Notre Dame.' Ophelia Grimm pointed towards the Île de la Cité, a small island in the middle of the Seine. 'Mr Trout has organized a practice session for himself on the organ in preparation for the performance and I thought we could listen while we tour the cathedral. I'm sure that his playing will be wonderful as always,' she said. 'Although I do hope he keeps that ridiculous hand waving to a minimum,' she whispered to herself.

Alice-Miranda and Millie overheard her and smiled. They both thought Mr Trout's extravagant organ playing was a highlight of each week's assembly.

The group continued walking until the top of an enormous building came into view.

'Is that it?' said Millie. Her eyes were on stalks.

'Yes, it certainly is,' Miss Reedy replied. The English teacher was walking right behind Millie and Alice-Miranda. 'It's gorgeous. And so much history. Did you know . . .?' Miss Reedy launched into one of her monologues, firing facts like a volley of cannonballs.

Millie loved looking at the buildings but, unlike Alice-Miranda, she wasn't especially interested in knowing every last detail. She decided that she would rather wait for Jacinta and Sloane than listen to Encyclopedia Reedy. She stopped to take a photo, while Alice-Miranda and Miss Reedy went ahead.

'Can you believe that we're really here?' Millie asked as she slid between the two older girls. 'Paris in the summer. It's lovely, isn't it?'

'My mother always promised that she'd take me

to Paris one day, but I doubt that's ever going to happen now, seeing that she and Daddy are getting divorced,' Jacinta huffed.

'But Jacinta, you're here in Paris, so she doesn't need to bring you,' said Millie, shaking her head. 'How is your mother, anyway?'

'Much better than I thought she'd be,' Jacinta replied. 'You know she's taken up gardening with Nosey Parker, which is a bit of a pain because Mrs Parker has turned up on the back doorstep every weekend that I've been home. She insists on me giving her a hug and a kiss and calling her Aunty Myrtle. It's horrible.' Jacinta shuddered, and then looked thoughtful. 'Sometimes I worry that Mummy will get tired of living in the village and start to look for a new husband. I'd like her to stay around now that we're finally getting to know each other better. She's quite good fun sometimes.'

Sloane and Millie nodded. Things between Jacinta and her mother had been tricky for as long as they'd known her. In recent months Jacinta's parents had separated. Her mother, Ambrosia, had settled in nearby Winchesterfield, where her once extravagant lifestyle was trimmed as tightly as a hedge at Queen Georgiana's palace.

'Maybe your mother will find a job to keep her busy,' Sloane suggested.

'Yeah, right,' Jacinta scoffed. 'I don't know what she could *do*, other than dressing up and looking glamorous, and she's way too old to start a modelling career now.'

'She might surprise you,' Sloane said. 'My mother still does the odd catalogue here and there.'

'And *you* said that it's totally embarrassing to see her parading around in nanna knickers for the entire world to see,' Jacinta retorted.

'Well, at least she's doing something,' Sloane hissed, 'which is more than I can say about *your* mother!'

Millie didn't like where the conversation was heading. Jacinta and Sloane had been so good lately. No one wanted to see a reappearance of their former selves. 'Have you been to Paris before, Sloane?' Millie asked quickly.

Sloane began to nod and then, thinking better of it, she shook her head. Sometimes old habits were hard to break and fibbing was the hardest of all. 'My mother hates Paris. Daddy brought her here when they were first married and Mummy imagined that it would be like her favourite old movie, *Roman*

Holiday, except in Paris, of course. But it was a huge disappointment. Daddy says that when he opened the door of their hotel room, Mummy shrieked and marched downstairs, yelling, "How dare you put us in a broom cupboard, that's just not on!"' Sloane imitated her mother, hands flying, hair bouncing.

Millie and Jacinta laughed. 'I wonder what our rooms will be like,' Sloane said. 'I'm not having a broom cupboard either, you know.'

'I don't think we'll have much choice,' said Millie. 'As long as there's a bed and a hot shower we really shouldn't complain. Unless you want to end up sleeping in a park.'

'Ha ha,' said Sloane. 'Miss Grimm wouldn't do that.'

Ophelia Grimm's ears pricked up on hearing her name. She turned and looked at the girls behind her. 'What wouldn't I do?'

Millie's stomach grumbled and she seized the chance to change the subject. 'Let us starve,' she said.

'Of course not, Millicent. As soon as we've toured the cathedral and heard Mr Trout's recital, we'll have lunch.' Miss Grimm had stopped on the path and was waiting for the group to catch up so they could cross the road together. 'I hope you like crepes.'

Millie licked her lips. 'Yum!'

The children walked in two lines along the footpath across the Pont d'Arcole, one of the numerous bridges that zigzagged across the river Seine. In the distance, the wailing of sirens grew louder and, as the group turned to see where the noise was coming from, a convoy of three police cars sped across the bridge beside them and skidded to a halt outside a townhouse.

'Cool,' one of the Fayle students, George 'Figgy' Figworth, called out.

'I wonder what's going on,' Millie said.

'Probably a murder,' Figgy replied.

'As if.' Sloane rolled her eyes.

Mr Plumpton overheard the young lad's comment. 'Master Figworth, I think you have a rather overactive imagination.'

Fayle student Rufus Pemberley added his two cents worth. 'Well, maybe someone stole that *Moaning Lisa* painting.'

'Goodness me, you two should be crime writers.' Mr Plumpton shook his head.

'And it's the *Mona Lisa*, Sherlock Holmes,' said Sloane. She pulled a face at Rufus.

'It's been stolen before, you know,' Figgy said.

'Some Italian guy just walked out with it and kept it for two years.'

Mr Plumpton frowned. 'Yes, that's true, Master Figworth. But how did *you* know that?'

'I read it somewhere,' the boy replied.

Mr Plumpton was impressed. Perhaps the lad was more of a scholar than people gave him credit for.

Miss Grimm led the group along the footpath towards the police cars that were now parked untidily across the road.

A tall man with salt-and-pepper hair rushed out of the front door of a townhouse. A young woman wearing a red and black polka dot skirt, white blouse and perilously high red heels followed behind him.

'*Nous avons été volés,*' the man shouted.

'What did he say?' Millie asked no one in particular.

'I think he just said that he'd been robbed,' Mr Plumpton replied.

'Cool,' Figgy said again.

'I don't think that fellow would agree with you.'

Miss Grimm wasn't keen to walk into the middle of a police investigation, so she led the children to the other side of the street.

'That poor man seems very upset,' Alice-Miranda commented to Miss Reedy. The child turned to look at him again. 'I think I've seen him somewhere before.'

'I don't recognize him,' Miss Reedy replied. 'But that doesn't mean much. You've met a lot of people, Alice-Miranda. It's entirely possible that you've come into contact with him before, knowing your parents' connections.'

One of the policemen pulled out a notebook and began to ask the man some questions.

By now the children were too far away to hear the conversation.

'Come along, everyone,' Miss Grimm turned and called to her charges. She was eager to get inside the cathedral and away from the drama outside. Police sirens and speeding cars were not on her list of sightseeing priorities.

Alice-Miranda's mind was ticking over as she tried to remember where she could have seen the grey-haired man. If Miss Grimm hadn't been in such a hurry she might have run back and introduced herself, even though her French wasn't very good. But the headmistress did not intend to stop.

The children, flanked by their teachers, walked into the cathedral. The drama outside was forgotten as an invisible cloak of silence wrapped around them.

Somewhere in the gallery, a boy began to sing; the purity of his voice sent shivers through the visitors below.

Alice-Miranda shuffled through the crowd to stand beside Millie. Both girls gazed up into the vast space.

'What do you think?' Alice-Miranda whispered.

'Oh my goodness, it's beautiful,' Millie gasped.

Chapter 3

Fabien Bouchard blinked. He rolled over, shielding his eyes from the bright light that flooded the room.

'No,' he groaned. 'I was having such a lovely dream.'

'What were you dreaming about this time?' his mother asked as she tied back the last curtain on the three double-height windows.

'Football,' Fabien answered.

'Oh my darling, football is for children and sweaty middle-aged men. At least you could dream about something important, like fashion. Half the day is gone and you have masterpieces to create,' she said.

The woman was dressed in tailored black pants and a simple black silk top. Her thick, ebony-coloured hair was pulled off her face in a low chignon and her pale face was free of make-up. Although there were some fine lines around the edges of her green eyes, she looked younger than her forty-three years.

'But I'm exhausted,' the boy sighed.

'I know you are, Fabien, but we must work hard to repay your uncle's kindness. If it weren't for him, I don't know where we would be.' The woman stood for a moment, staring out of the window and onto the street below.

Fabien sat up and watched her. 'Mama, are you all right?'

She spun around and walked over to the enormous bed, then perched on its edge. 'Of course. It's just that there have been so many sacrifices, Fabien. But soon you will have everything you have ever wanted.'

All he wanted was to go home to Guernsey. He doubted that was what she meant.

She leaned down and kissed him on the forehead. 'You need to get up and make your mama proud.'

'Will you come to the show?' he asked excitedly.

She pulled away and crossed her arms in front of her. 'I'm sorry but it's just not possible. Maybe one day.'

Fabien's face fell.

'Please don't look like that,' she begged.

Fabien pushed himself back against the pillows. 'I shouldn't have asked. Now you're upset.'

'No, I am not upset, Fabien. I just can't come. That's all. Now, hurry up. The day is wasting and I need to talk to you about some of the designs. Your Uncle Claude will be back soon.'

She hurried from the room.

Fabien threw off the covers and swivelled his feet to the floor. He pulled on some trousers and a shirt without even pausing to admire their beautiful cut and cloth, and followed his mother down the hall.

'Now tell me, Fabien, what is this we have used on the bodice?' she asked when he caught up to her. They stood in a large room surrounded by mannequins dressed in splendid gowns.

'Lace,' he said.

Neither Fabien nor his mother heard Claude's silent footsteps as he entered the room.

'Of course it's lace,' the man snapped. Fabien and

his mother jumped like startled cats. 'Any buffoon knows that. Your mother wants to know what type of lace it is.'

'Bonjour, monsieur.' Sybilla moved across the room and kissed her brother on both cheeks. 'It's good to have you home again.'

'*Oui*, I am glad to be home. These business trips are so tiresome,' he sighed, then raised his eyebrows. 'But profitable.' The man turned his attention back to Fabien. 'Now, answer your mother. What type of lace is that?'

The young man hesitated. 'Chantilly?'

Madame Bouchard sighed deeply and glanced at her brother. 'No. It's Venetian. From the finest Italian lace makers. Have I taught you nothing, my son?'

'I just draw the pictures, Mama. I don't know why I need to have a thousand fabrics catalogued in my head too,' Fabien complained.

His uncle snorted. 'If you want to be the world's most important designer, you need to know more than that, dear boy.'

'I never said that *I* wanted to be the world's most important designer. You did.'

The man stiffened. 'You have more talent in your little finger than most people have in their whole body and yet you taunt us, Fabien. Don't you want to be someone? To make your mark on this world? To show them.'

Fabien wondered who his uncle meant by 'them' but he didn't dare ask.

'Now listen to your mother and learn.' Claude glanced at his watch.

'Are you going out again?' Sybilla asked.

'*Oui*. Is there anything you need before I go?'

'The green satin; I am ready to cut the pattern,' she replied.

'I will bring it up,' he offered.

'Where are you going, Uncle Claude?' Fabien wished his uncle would offer to take him too.

'That is not for you to be concerned about. It's just business.' He stalked out of the room, leaving Fabien and Sybilla to their work.

'Come along, darling. We will make some notes and then Uncle Claude will be pleased. You know he loves us very much,' said Sybilla as she patted her son on the arm.

Fabien knew that. It's just that sometimes he wished things were different.

Chapter 4

Alice-Miranda noticed that Sloane was limping. 'Are you all right?'

Sloane shook her head and stumbled as she tried to keep up with the rest of the group. 'My feet hurt.'

At the head of the line, Professor Winterbottom, the headmaster of Fayle, and Mr Grump, Miss Grimm's husband, were maintaining a brisk pace on their way to the hotel from Notre Dame.

'I've got a blister,' Sloane complained, then suddenly knelt down in the middle of the path to inspect it. Ophelia Grimm, who was marching along behind and looking at the scenery, almost tripped over her.

'Sloane! Don't just stop like that. It's dangerous,' the headmistress admonished. She straightened herself up and studied Sloane's silver sandals. 'Perhaps you should have thought about wearing more sensible shoes. I warned you that we'd be walking quite a distance today. It's the best way to orientate yourself in a new city.'

Deidre Winterbottom stopped beside Sloane. 'Now let me take a look, dear.' The headmaster's wife examined Sloane's feet before reaching into her giant backpack and producing an astonishing array of bandaids. 'Good gracious, it's a miracle you could walk at all with the size of that monster,' Mrs Winterbottom noted.

Within a few seconds, Sloane's left heel was sporting a large plaster and her right had a smaller covering.

'Thank you, Mrs Winterbottom,' Sloane said.

'That must feel better already,' said Alice-Miranda, as she reached out to hold Sloane's hand.

'I don't know why we couldn't have taken the bus back,' the older girl grouched as she limped along.

She wished she'd worn her own footwear instead of borrowing brand new shoes from Jacinta.

'It's not much further now,' the headmistress confirmed. 'Just around the corner.'

Sloane looked worried. Miss Grimm's 'just around the corner' was usually at least another mile, but this time she was pleasantly surprised. Professor Winterbottom turned onto a narrow road and there in front of them was l'Hôtel Lulu.

To the right of the front door, a delicate pair of ornate iron gates led into a courtyard. Professor Winterbottom guided the children inside, where they quickly sat on the wooden benches lining the enclosure. The small space was beautifully decorated with a lion's head wall fountain and rows of red geraniums. Miss Grimm and Mrs Winterbottom headed into reception to sort out the rooms and keys.

Sloane took off her shoes as soon as she was seated.

'Does anyone know what we're having for dinner tonight?' called Rufus Pemberley.

'Yeah, I could eat a horse,' Figgy added.

'Be careful what you wish for,' Sep grinned. 'The French eat horses, you know.'

'Really?' Figgy grimaced. 'Then again, I suppose it's just like eating a cow.'

Jacinta shuddered. 'Oh, disgusting. I'm sure that's not true.'

'It is, Jacinta,' Alice-Miranda replied. 'Lots of people around the world eat horses. I can't imagine it, though – I'd just see Bony staring up at me from the plate, or Rockstar or Chops. I couldn't do it, I'm afraid, and I've eaten quite a lot of unusual things.'

'We'll be walking to a restaurant not far from here,' Mr Grump informed the children. 'We'll meet back here at six thirty, once you've settled into your rooms.'

'Not *more* walking,' Sloane whined.

'What sort of food are we really having?' Jacinta asked tentatively, hoping Sep had been kidding about the horses.

'Just the usual French delicacies. You know, snails, frogs' legs, that sort of thing,' said Mr Grump. He laughed as the children squirmed.

Sloane pulled a face. 'I'm not eating any of that.'

'Me neither,' Jacinta agreed.

'Frogs' legs are delicious, Jacinta,' Alice-Miranda said. 'They taste a bit like chicken. And snails are not as rubbery as you might think.'

'Count me out for both. I'm not eating Kermit and I'd rather chew on a rubber band than eat a snail,' Sloane quipped.

'I'll try snails.' Figgy was now pretending to put his finger up his nose. 'They probably taste like snot, Jacinta, and I'm sure you know what that's like. Mmm, salty.' He licked his lips.

'You are *disgusting*,' Sloane wailed.

'Figworth, you can stop that nonsense right now,' said Professor Winterbottom, glaring at the lad. Sometimes he wondered if the boy had a brain at all inside that boofy head of his. Who would have guessed that Fayle's star second rower, a veritable giant of a lad, had the voice of an angel?

'It's all right, Jacinta. There will be plenty of regular food on the menu too,' said Mr Grump. He'd decided he had better not upset the children too much. He didn't want to get into trouble with his wife.

It wasn't long before Miss Grimm and Mrs Winterbottom reappeared holding a handful of plastic hotel keys.

'Can I have everyone's attention, please?' called Miss Grimm. 'Children, you will be sharing two to a room. Each of you will have your own key. Please don't lose them. Girls will be on the second and third floors and boys on the fourth and fifth with teachers interspersed throughout. I will give you a list of room numbers for the teachers, who will be available should you need anything. I *don't* expect to find girls on the boys' floors or vice versa. Is that understood?' Miss Grimm smiled at her young charges.

'Yes, Miss Grimm,' the children chorused.

'The rooms have been allocated at random. I know that some are larger than others but I have no idea which is which. It's simply the luck of the draw.' Miss Grimm scanned the list in her hand. 'Alice-Miranda, you're sharing with Millie in room 201 . . . Jacinta, you and Sloane are together in room 202 . . .'

The girls stepped forward to receive their keys. Mr Grump and Mr Plumpton showed them to the storeroom to collect their luggage and with military precision Miss Grimm had everyone in their rooms within fifteen minutes.

'I wonder if there's a view,' said Millie. She pulled back the curtains to reveal a wall. 'Ahh, no, not unless you're a fan of old bricks.'

'It doesn't matter,' said Alice-Miranda as she opened her suitcase. 'I'm sure we won't be here very much anyway. It sounds like Miss Grimm has a busy schedule arranged.'

The room was tiny, with two single beds, a chest of drawers and a bathroom that just fitted a shower, toilet and basin. The minute window opened only a fraction and there was barely enough room for the girls to drag their suitcases around the floor.

'Sloane will be whining her head off if their room is the same as ours,' Millie said.

There was a loud knock on the door.

Alice-Miranda opened it and Sloane and Jacinta rushed into the room, tripping over Alice-Miranda's suitcase and sprawling side by side onto her bed.

The girls laughed as Jacinta performed a dainty forward roll only to find herself wedged between the two beds.

She propped herself up on her elbows, looking like an otter with its head poking out of the sea.

'So, this is *your* room?' Sloane said, as she and Jacinta traded broad smiles.

'Yes. It's small, but perfectly formed,' Alice-Miranda replied.

'Seriously? It's just small, Alice-Miranda,' Jacinta scoffed.

'Why? What's your room like?' Millie asked.

'It's a mansion compared to this one,' said Sloane smugly.

'Come on then, let's see.' Millie grabbed Jacinta's hand to help her out of the tight spot and the girls charged off across the hallway.

Sloane swiped the key and opened the door to reveal a huge sitting room complete with two lounge chairs, a small coffee table and a fireplace. Through another doorway was a double bedroom, with not one but two double beds and a bathroom with a large spa.

Millie was gobsmacked. 'Wow! This is ridiculous.'

'It's lovely,' Alice-Miranda said.

Both rooms had views of the street too.

'I suppose I can't complain about being in a broom cupboard now, can I?' Sloane said. 'Although you two could.'

'You wouldn't want to. Miss Grimm would soon find you one.' Millie giggled. 'Her room's probably not nearly as good as this. Don't let her in or she might want to swap.'

Alice-Miranda shook her head. 'Miss Grimm wouldn't do that. Well, not unless we suggest it.' She winked at Millie.

'What?' Sloane's mouth gaped open. 'I always thought you were the only truly nice person I'd ever met Alice-Miranda.'

'Hey! What about us?' Millie looked at Jacinta and the two of them glared at Sloane.

'You know what I mean,' Sloane replied. 'Alice-Miranda's, like, weirdly nice. You're just normal nice.'

Alice-Miranda grinned. 'I wouldn't really tell. Anyway, Miss Grimm said it was just the luck of the draw whoever got the best rooms, and I think you two won the lottery this time.'

Chapter 5

Upstairs, Sep and Lucas were busy sorting out their things when Sep realized that his backpack was missing. He thought he'd left it down in the courtyard and so went to ask Mr Lipp if he could collect it.

The boy flew down the stairs two at a time and was relieved to spy his backpack, which contained his camera and wallet, beside the bench he'd been sitting on. As he picked up the bag, he was distracted by a voice coming from the street.

He walked towards the iron gates to take a look.

Across the road a wiry man wearing a black beret was speaking in French with the odd English word in between. Sep looked to see who he was talking to, then realized the man was on the telephone. He didn't sound happy at all.

'*Pas chinchilla! Vigogne, tu comprends?*'

The man finished the conversation and jammed the phone into his trouser pocket. Then he walked around to the boot of a black sedan and popped it open. He leaned in and picked up a long roll of something. Sep thought it might have been a rug.

The man carried the roll down a set of stairs into a basement before returning to the car and picking up another one.

Sep's shoes crunched on the gravel and the man looked up and spotted him. The fellow stared at Sep and then slowly nodded his head.

Sep gave a small wave. He felt as if he'd just seen something he shouldn't have, although he couldn't say what. Something about the pointy-looking fellow made him feel very uncomfortable. He scurried back inside the hotel.

'*Bonjour.*' A tall, thickset man with glasses emerged from a door marked '*Privé:* Private'. He walked behind a woman sitting at the reception desk and out into the foyer. A small copper-coloured dog followed close at his heels.

'*Bonjour*,' Sep replied. He reached down and held out his hand to the dog. She sniffed it, put her nose in the air and trotted over to her master.

'Don't mind Lulu. She is a terrible snob. You must give her something to eat.' The man spoke English with a thick French accent. 'Then she will be your friend.'

'What sort of dog is she?' Sep replied.

'Spoiled,' said the woman.

'*Bonjour*, madame,' Sep greeted her.

'*Bonjour*, young man. You are with the singers?' she asked.

Sep nodded. 'I'm Sep.'

'Welcome, Sep. I hope you enjoy your stay,' she said. 'I am Madame Crabbe and he is Monsieur Crabbe. And that snooty creature there is his baby, Lulu. She is a miniature dachshund.'

'The hotel is called Lulu, isn't it?' Sep asked.

'*Oui*. Monsieur Crabbe is obsessed. Sometimes I think he loves that dog first and me second,' said Madame Crabbe, pouting.

'That is not true, my dear. I love Lulu, then I love my accordion and then I love you,' Monsieur Crabbe said with a wink at Sep. 'But this boy did not come to Paris to hear our bickering.'

'At least there is always Monsieur Lawrence,' said Madame Crabbe. She pulled a framed picture from the cabinet behind the counter. 'See?' She thrust it forward for Sep to look at.

Sep walked towards her and studied the photograph. Madame Crabbe was standing beside Lawrence Ridley with a beaming smile on her face.

'I know him,' Sep said.

'You do not!' Madame Crabbe exclaimed.

'Yes, I really do. My best friend is his son and he's married to the aunt of another of my friends. They're both here in the hotel. My friends, I mean,' Sep explained.

'*Sacré bleu*, he is married and he has a son?' Madame Crabbe frowned. 'How did I not know this?'

'They kept the wedding pretty quiet. It was on Aunty Gee's ship, the *Octavia*. I couldn't believe I got to go.'

Madame Crabbe sighed loudly.

Monsieur Crabbe tutted and shook his head. 'You are a dreamer, my love.'

'I know. And mostly I dream of Monsieur Lawrence, you big oaf.' She turned her attention back to Sep. 'I met him last year when he was filming just around the corner. I ran into him in the street and almost fainted. I was so overcome – he gave me his arm to steady myself and then he agreed to have his photograph taken with me. He is so handsome.' Madame Crabbe sighed again.

Sep laughed. 'You sound just like my friend Jacinta. She loves him too. I'll get Lucas and Alice-Miranda to stop in and say hello when we go out later,' Sep offered.

'I can have a photograph with the children too, perhaps?' asked Madame Crabbe. Her husband snorted. She reached up and pinched her husband's cheek. 'You must remind me again why I am married to you.'

'Because I am handsome.' Monsieur Crabbe ran his fingers down his neck. 'And strong.' He flexed his right arm. 'And no one else would have you.'

Madame Crabbe rolled her eyes at Sep. 'Don't mind him. I know he loves me.'

Sep grinned. Madame and Monsieur Crabbe were funny and he had forgotten all about the pointy little man across the road.

Chapter 6

That evening, Miss Grimm and Mr Grump led the children to a traditional French restaurant called *Christophe*, which was a short walk from the hotel. Jacinta and Sloane were horrified to find snails and frogs' legs on the menu but relieved to learn that they could order whatever they liked. Both girls settled on the salmon and found it to be delicious.

The group was spread across four round tables with the teachers interspersed throughout. Miss Reedy had joined Alice-Miranda, Millie, Sep,

Lucas, Jacinta and Sloane. She was indicating to Mr Plumpton that he should join them too when, out of nowhere, Mr Lipp appeared and slid into the vacant chair beside her. Mr Plumpton frowned but retreated silently to the table opposite with Mr Trout.

From where she sat, Alice-Miranda had a clear view of her Science teacher, and he hadn't taken his eyes off Miss Reedy since they sat down.

'So, Livinia.' Harry Lipp leaned in towards Miss Reedy and twirled the end of his handlebar moustache. 'Have you had any thoughts on our selection for next year's joint play?'

Miss Reedy sat up straighter in her chair. 'No, not yet. It's still a long way off and I have all sorts of end-of-year celebrations to get through first.'

'Well, I just thought we could spend some time together over the next week – you know what they say, two heads are better than one.' Mr Lipp grinned at her and winked.

Livinia Reedy blushed. 'No, I . . . I'm sure that we're going to be very busy and I have a huge pile of marking to get through. I had to bring it with me. There won't be any spare time at all.'

'We'll see.' Mr Lipp picked up his napkin and accidentally brushed the side of Miss Reedy's hand.

Her face turned the colour of an overripe tomato.

Millie had been watching the exchange too. 'I think Hairy Lipp's making moves on Miss Reedy,' she whispered to Alice-Miranda behind her hand.

'Oh no, poor Mr Plumpton,' Alice-Miranda replied. 'If he doesn't hurry up and tell her how he feels, he might lose her.'

'But not to Hairy Lipp. He's weird,' Millie said with a grimace.

'Perhaps we should try to help Mr Lipp find someone more suitable,' Alice-Miranda suggested, raising her eyebrows playfully.

Millie looked around at the rest of the group. 'I don't think Miss Grimm or Mrs Winterbottom will have the slightest interest.'

'I didn't mean them,' Alice-Miranda said. 'Perhaps he'll meet a lovely French lady while we're here.'

'Like that waitress.' Millie pointed at a very pretty young woman who was clearing the plates from the table opposite them. 'She looks nice.'

'I don't suppose anyone ever knows where or when they might meet the love of their life,' Alice-Miranda said. 'And Paris seems like the perfect place to fall in love.'

'That's so true,' Jacinta sighed, while staring at Lucas.

Millie shook her head. 'You're a hopeless case, you know.'

'I know.' Jacinta nodded absently.

The children ate their meals with great gusto. They were just finishing their desserts when Cornelius Trout approached Miss Grimm and Mr Grump. He leaned down and spoke to Ophelia in hushed tones, gesturing towards a grand piano in the corner of the room.

'I can't see why not. Why don't you ask the owner?' said Miss Grimm.

Cornelius Trout headed over to the front desk and returned, nodding emphatically.

Miss Grimm stood up and looked around the group. 'Children, Mr Trout has arranged an impromptu performance for you.'

The restaurant owner stepped forward and explained to the other patrons in French.

An elderly man and woman smiled broadly as Cornelius ushered the children into the space beside the piano. Mr Lipp took his position to conduct the choir.

The music teacher placed his hands on the keys and began an impressive introduction, which silenced the chatter in the room. The first song in their repertoire was a beautiful Rutter piece called 'For the Beauty of the Earth', followed by a snappy medley of songs from *Sister Act* that soon had the patrons humming along. Their final chorus for the night was a particularly animated version of the old Elton John classic 'Don't Go Breaking My Heart', in which Figgy and Susannah had solos. They both hammed it up, much to the delight of everyone watching.

As they finished their last tune, the patrons clapped and cheered. The children took a bow just as Mr Lipp had taught them and Cornelius Trout stood up from the piano and acknowledged the applause.

'That was fun,' Jacinta whispered. 'I hope all the shows are as good as that.'

'We'll rehearse your solo tomorrow, Jacinta,' Mr Lipp said and smiled at her.

Jacinta nodded. She had been surprised to get the part in the first place. Now, after visiting Notre Dame that morning, she was terrified by the prospect of singing on her own in the cathedral, even if it was only one verse.

Sloane felt a twinge in her tummy. She had wanted that part but hadn't been game enough to audition. It wasn't fair. Jacinta was a gymnastics superstar and now she was going to be a singing sensation too. Sloane wondered if she'd ever get a chance to be in the spotlight – for something good.

'Well done,' Professor Winterbottom called as the children returned to their seats.

'Yes, good work everyone,' Miss Grimm added. 'But I think we should be getting back to the hotel. It's almost bedtime and we have a busy day of sight-seeing tomorrow.'

'Hopefully we won't be walking everywhere,' Sloane whispered.

'And we'll be travelling on foot, so please make sure that you wear appropriate shoes.' Miss Grimm arched an eyebrow at Sloane. 'If I were you, young lady, I'd bring a good supply of bandaids.'

'Yes, Miss Grimm,' Sloane muttered.

The group trotted back to the hotel in high spirits and assembled in the foyer.

'We'll see everyone down here for breakfast at half past seven,' Professor Winterbottom informed the children. 'And I expect all of you to have showers and wash properly, and brush your teeth. Yes, I'm looking at you, Rufus Pemberley.' The headmaster glared at the lad, whose hair resembled a bird's nest.

'Tomorrow we will visit several historic sites . . .' Miss Grimm began.

Miss Reedy was standing to the side fidgeting with her hands. 'Oh dear me,' she said.

'Is everything all right, Miss Reedy?' asked Alice-Miranda, who was standing next to her.

'I think I've left my camera at the restaurant,' the teacher explained. 'I'd best pop back and get it before they close.'

'I'll come with you,' Mr Lipp offered. He hadn't left the woman's side since they'd departed from the restaurant.

Miss Reedy shook her head. 'Oh, no, I'll be fine.'

'I insist,' said Mr Lipp. 'It's not right for a lady to be out on her own at this time of night.'

'Mr Lipp, it's half past eight and it's still daylight. I'm sure that I can walk a few hundred metres without finding myself in mortal danger,' Miss Reedy rebuffed.

'I'm sure you can, Miss Reedy. But I wouldn't be a gentleman if I didn't offer.'

The English teacher looked cornered.

'Miss Reedy, may I speak with you in private?' Alice-Miranda asked.

'Yes, of course.' Miss Reedy removed herself

from Mr Lipp and wondered at the reason for her youngest student's serious face.

'Perhaps we could talk outside?' The tiny child pointed at the glass doors that led from the foyer to the courtyard. Meanwhile, Miss Grimm was waxing lyrical about the Louvre Museum and the Eiffel Tower and myriad other landmarks on the tour list.

Miss Reedy looked puzzled. 'Is everything all right, Alice-Miranda?'

'Yes, I just thought you might like me to go with you to the restaurant. I'm sure that we can be there and back before anyone's had time to miss us,' she suggested.

'Oh, sweet girl.' Miss Reedy smiled. 'That would be lovely.'

Inside, Harry Lipp craned his neck to see what was happening in the courtyard.

The headmistress interrupted his thoughts. 'Mr Lipp, would you like to explain the rehearsal schedule before I give the full details for tomorrow's activities.'

'What?' he grunted.

'The rehearsal schedule, Mr Lipp. That is your domain, isn't it?' Ophelia Grimm sometimes wondered what planet Harry Lipp had descended from. And as for his choice of clothing! It was a constant source of wonder to her. Here in Paris, where one tried one's best to blend in and look as chic as the locals, she could only hope that Harry had left his brightest ensembles at home.

Livinia Reedy and Alice-Miranda set off and, just as the child predicted, they were at the restaurant and back before Miss Grimm had finished outlining the next day's tour.

Chapter 7

Fabien Bouchard sat at the drawing board, tapping his pencil against the blank sheet of paper. Some days the ideas flowed like a river and others, such as today, there wasn't even a trickle. A pile of unopened magazines sat stacked in the corner of the room. His uncle said that he should use them for inspiration but Fabien refused to look. The critics had said his first collection was wholly original. Fabien was scared that if he looked at what everyone else was doing he might be tempted, in difficult times, to follow their lead.

Right now he was stuck. He hopped down from the chair and pulled a small suitcase out from under the bed. He lifted it onto the bedclothes and snapped the locks, revealing a set of sketchpads. Drawing had always been the one thing he was good at. Even when he was very young and struggled to learn to read, he could always draw.

Then, a few years ago, he had started sketching dresses. He couldn't even say why. They were just images that would come to him, often in dreams. After a while, he began to put them down on paper. It was his secret until one day Uncle Claude came to visit and saw them sitting on his desk. Everything changed after that. Sometimes Fabien wished he'd kept the drawings hidden. But it was much too late for regrets. And besides, he loved seeing his creations come to life, especially when sewn by his mother's deft hands.

Last year, Uncle Claude had brought Fabien across for the first ever showing of his designs. Then, a few months ago, Uncle Claude said that the business was getting too big for him to trek back and forth between Paris and Guernsey. It would be far easier for everyone if Fabien and his mother moved to the city, at least for the time being.

After the quiet life he and his mother had led on the island in the middle of the English Channel, Fabien found the idea appealing. Fabien always knew that his mother struggled socially. He had never been allowed to bring friends home from school and she had always kept to herself in the village. Of course, it had been difficult for her because she had refused to learn more than a few words of English. She left the house only to go to the market and never made any friends. Fabien always thought she was just terribly shy. He hoped that moving to Paris would inspire her to get out more. Surely once she was back in France she would live a little, Fabien had thought.

But as soon as they had arrived in Paris, Sybilla refused to leave the house at all. Claude had taken Fabien aside and told him that his mother was unwell. She suffered terribly with a condition called agoraphobia and she was getting worse. Uncle Claude said that even the thought of going outside would make her ill and, to make matters worse, a kind of paranoia had overcome her. She had told Claude she was terrified that if Fabien left the house alone, something awful would happen to him. Uncle Claude promised Fabien that he would get the best doctors. He told the boy that she would not take her medication so it was up to him to help and make sure that when his uncle was away, Fabien mixed the medicine into her food. But she could not know – she was getting sicker and didn't realize it.

Uncle Claude said that she would get better but for now, Fabien must stay at home with her at all times, or there might be an episode. His uncle told him not to ask her about it either – the mere mention of her health might be enough to tip Sybilla over the edge. Fabien loved his mother more than anyone in the world. His father had abandoned her when she was pregnant with him, so along with Uncle Claude they were the only family he had. He would do anything to keep her safe; even if it meant being imprisoned at home until she was well again. But he was finding it harder each day.

His uncle had made his fortune selling exquisite handmade rugs from the Middle East. The townhouse floors were covered with them. Fabien's mother always said that her brother was a clever businessman. He looked after them financially and made sure that they had everything they needed. But now he was obsessed with making Fabien a star, whether Fabien wanted it or not.

The young man exhaled deeply. Life could have been worse, he told himself. At least his mother was here with him and Uncle Claude, though sometimes demanding, only wanted what was best for them all. Fabien closed his eyes. An image of a beautiful gown with a voluminous skirt began to form. His pencil flew across the page. For now he must focus on his work and on helping his mother to get well.

Chapter 8

Alice-Miranda and Millie had both slept soundly. They were up, showered and dressed long before the appointed breakfast time of half past seven.

Millie finished flicking through the mini guide to Paris that her grandfather had given her just before she left. She put it into her backpack and decided to go and see how Sloane and Jacinta were getting on.

Alice-Miranda was fiddling with her camera, making sure that the battery had charged properly.

'I've got my key,' Millie said.

Alice-Miranda laughed. 'I'd let you in, you know.'

Millie grinned. 'It's fun being tourists, isn't it? I feel so grown up having my own hotel key, even if it is just a white plastic card.'

Alice-Miranda nodded. 'When we're older, I think we should go on a huge adventure. We could hike in the Andes or study giant tortoises on the Galapagos Islands or walk the Great Wall of China.'

'We could have a gap year like my cousin Amelia did,' Millie agreed. 'But you know, we'll probably have to take Sloane and Jacinta too, or we'll never hear the end of it.'

'I'd love them to come,' said Alice-Miranda.

'I don't think backpacking would be Sloane's thing, though. We'd need to hire a whole village of Sherpas just to carry her suitcases,' Millie commented. 'And Jacinta isn't exactly into camping either.'

Millie disappeared into the hallway and reappeared a minute later. 'We might want to rethink our gap-year plans,' she said.

'What do you mean?' Alice-Miranda frowned.

'I woke them up and now they're having a huge row about whose fault it was that the alarm didn't go off. And overnight that gigantic suite of theirs has been invaded by the Paris clothes monster, which I think vomited all over their floor.'

'Oh no.' Alice-Miranda's eyes were wide. 'It sounds like they could do with some help.'

Millie screwed up her nose. 'I'm not going back in there. It's dangerous. And I don't mean the monster.'

Miss Grimm was now marching up and down the hallway and knocking on doors to warn the girls that she would be inspecting their rooms in ten minutes.

'Come on, Millie, I don't want Miss Grimm starting the day in a bad mood, do you?' Alice-Miranda gave her friend a gentle shove and they scurried across the hallway. Alice-Miranda knocked loudly on the door to room 202 and waited.

'I'm coming,' Jacinta called from inside. She wrenched open the door.

'Good morning,' Alice-Miranda greeted her. 'Millie and I have come to see if you need any help.'

'I haven't,' Millie scoffed from behind her.

Alice-Miranda turned around. 'You don't mean that,' she mouthed, and then turned back to Jacinta, who did the strangest thing. She grabbed Alice-Miranda and hugged her tightly.

'Yes, please.' A tear spilled onto Jacinta's cheek. She released her tiny friend and retreated inside.

'It can't be as bad as all . . .' Alice-Miranda began to say, then stopped when she caught sight of the sitting room. Millie was right. There were clothes from one end of the place to the other.

'Was there a bomb in your suitcase or something?' Millie said bluntly.

Jacinta sighed. 'I don't know. It just sort of happened.'

Alice-Miranda began to pick up various garments from the floor. 'Come on, it won't take more than a few minutes to get this sorted out.' She walked over to Jacinta's black suitcase and upended the rest of the overflowing contents onto the couch. 'Are you ready to go?' she asked Jacinta.

'I just have to brush my hair and find some shoes,' she answered.

'OK, you go and do that and Millie and I will make a start here,' Alice-Miranda reassured her.

Jacinta disappeared into the bedroom.

'Tell Sloane to hurry up too,' Millie shouted after her. She could still hear the shower going.

By the time Miss Grimm knocked on the door, Alice-Miranda and Millie had completely sorted out

Jacinta and Sloane's mess and returned to their own room. The two older girls looked sheepish as the headmistress inspected their suite.

'I must say, girls, that I am pleasantly surprised,' said Miss Grimm with a smile. 'Well done. It's a lovely room and it looks as though you are quite deserving of it. Now, make sure that you have everything you need for the day and I will see you downstairs in a minute.'

As Miss Grimm was halfway out the door, she poked her head back inside. 'And Sloane –' She studied the child's sensible trainers. 'Good shoes.'

A few moments later, Miss Grimm had finished her inspection of Millie and Alice-Miranda's room and moved down the hallway to see Susannah and Ashima.

The four friends met at the top of the stairs.

'How was your inspection?' Millie asked, raising her eyebrows.

'Fine, thank you,' Jacinta mumbled, casting her eyes to the floor.

Sloane grinned tightly. 'Yeah, thanks for that.'

'We were happy to help,' Alice-Miranda said.

'Speak for yourself. But I told Miss Grimm how hopeless you both are and that we had to rescue you,' said Millie, deadpan.

Jacinta and Sloane gulped in unison.

'Millie!' Alice-Miranda admonished. 'She did not.'

Millie laughed. 'That had you worried, didn't it?'

'It's all right, we promise it won't happen again,' said Jacinta. She eyeballed her roommate. 'Will it, Sloane?'

'No, it won't,' she spat back.

'Come on, you two, please don't fight,' said Alice-Miranda. 'Tomorrow morning, as soon as Millie or I get up, we'll give you a wake-up call and make sure that you don't miss the alarm. Then you'll have plenty of time to get organized.'

'So, I'll just reset the alarm for half past five, shall I?' Millie asked.

'No way!' Sloane grouched.

'Better make it half past four then, Millie,' Jacinta grinned. 'It takes that long for Sloane to have a shower.'

Sloane turned around and poked out her tongue.

Alice-Miranda raised her nose in the air and drew in a deep breath. 'I'm starving and I can smell breakfast. Let's go.'

The girls headed downstairs. Fortunately, a tasty selection of croissants and pastries and the promise of a fun day ahead seemed to sweeten Sloane's and Jacinta's moods considerably. By the time the group left for the Louvre, they were chatting away as happily as they ever had.

Chapter 9

Miss Reedy snapped a photograph of the whole group standing beside the large glass pyramid in the forecourt of the Louvre. The enormous Louvre had once been a palace but was now the most famous museum and art gallery in the world.

'It says here that it was added to the museum in 1989,' Millie read from her guidebook. 'I'm not sure about the two smaller ones, but they were probably built at the same time.'

'I think they look weird,' Jacinta said.

'Ugly, did you say?' Sloane added.

'They're certainly interesting,' said Alice-Miranda. 'And really different from the original buildings.'

'We'll be heading inside for a private guided tour,' Miss Grimm informed the group. 'Please stay together and if you do find yourself separated from the others, just ask anyone with a badge on and they will take you to the central meeting place.'

The children nodded.

'Did you hear what I said, Mr Lipp?' Miss Grimm asked the teacher, who seemed to be staring into the distance at something – or someone.

'Sorry, Miss Grimm, what was that?' he said.

'Never mind. You're a big boy, I'm sure you can look after yourself,' said Miss Grimm. She'd decided there was no way he could get lost today, dressed in that mustard-coloured suit and bright pink cravat.

The children and teachers entered the enormous foyer. Alice-Miranda wandered over to speak to her Science teacher, who seemed lost in his thoughts. Millie joined them. 'Are you enjoying the trip so far, Mr Plumpton?'

'Oh, hello there, girls. Yes, yes it's marvellous,' he replied.

'Is there anything in particular you're looking forward to seeing in here?' Alice-Miranda asked.

'The *Mona Lisa*, of course,' said Josiah Plumpton. 'Leonardo da Vinci is something of a hero of mine.'

'I didn't realize you were interested in art,' Millie said.

'Mr da Vinci wasn't just an artist, Millicent. He was a scientist and an inventor, an architect and a musician, among many other things,' Mr Plumpton explained.

'Oh, yes,' Alice-Miranda piped up. 'Can you believe he designed flying machines? His anatomical drawings were incredible too.'

'Ah, I see we have a common interest,' said Mr Plumpton, with a twinkle in his eye.

'Yes, sir. My father is a huge fan too. Whenever there is an exhibition he usually takes me along,' explained Alice-Miranda. 'If ever anyone invents time travel, I think Daddy would be the first in line to go back and meet him.'

'I couldn't agree more,' Mr Plumpton said.

'What are you two agreeing on?' Miss Reedy asked as she joined the trio. That morning she had found herself monopolized once again by Mr Lipp. She had only just escaped, after Mr Trout had decided that he and Mr Lipp needed to discuss some of the finer points of rehearsals.

'Alice-Miranda and Mr Plumpton have been comparing notes about Leonardo da Vinci,' said Millie.

'Yes, what a genius. I'm so looking forward to seeing the *Mona Lisa* this morning,' Miss Reedy said.

'You should walk with Mr Plumpton, then,' Alice-Miranda suggested. 'He's an expert on Mr da Vinci.'

'Oh, Alice-Miranda, I think you're overstating things there. You seem to know an awful lot yourself.'

'Yeah, you know heaps,' Millie told Alice-Miranda.

'No, Millie, Mr Plumpton knows so much *more* than I do. Miss Reedy would love to have such special- ist knowledge, don't you think?' Alice-Miranda gave Millie a meaningful look.

Millie frowned. 'Oh! Yes, of course. Miss Reedy, you should stay with Mr Plumpton. For the whole tour.'

'You're welcome to come with us too,' Miss Reedy replied.

'No, didn't you have some things you wanted to talk to Mr Lipp about, Alice-Miranda?' Millie asked her friend.

'Yes, absolutely. I've wanted to get his attention all morning but he's been so preoccupied. Let's go and see him now, shall we?' Alice-Miranda looked at Mr Plumpton and gave him a cheeky wink.

The man's nose glowed red and he looked for a moment as if he might pass out.

'See you later then, girls,' said Miss Reedy. She felt a shy smile perch on her lips as she turned to Mr Plumpton.

'Well, there are a few things I'd like to know about Mr da Vinci, if you'd be happy enough to allow me to accompany you.'

He bowed his head ever so slightly. 'I'd be delighted.'

Miss Reedy blushed.

A few metres away, Mr Grump and Professor Winterbottom appeared with a lady dressed in a smart uniform.

'Gather around, everyone,' the professor called. 'This is our tour guide, Brigitte. Be sure to watch her and listen to all her instructions.'

'*Bonjour*,' Brigitte smiled.

'*Bonjour*,' the group chorused.

'Now, we have a lot to cover this morning and I would like to get to as many of the exhibits as possible . . .'

Alice-Miranda and Millie hovered close to Mr Lipp and Mr Trout, ready to swoop. They were quite certain they had enough questions to keep the man busy for the whole tour.

Chapter 10

After two hours wandering through the world's most incredible collection of art works, Brigitte led the group back to the cloakroom where the children collected their bags and awaited their next instructions.

Millie and Alice-Miranda hadn't needed to use their intervention skills as Mr Trout had chewed Mr Lipp's ear for the entire tour. The girls had hovered for a while, then upon deciding that Miss Reedy would be safe, they'd strolled about enjoying the art.

'Well, the *Mona Lisa* was a *big* disappointment,' Sloane announced.

'Why do you say that?' Alice-Miranda asked.

'It's so small. I was expecting something huge. And she's got such a strange look on her face. As if she was expecting your room at the hotel and she got ours instead,' Sloane said.

Alice-Miranda and Millie laughed.

'I suppose that's one way of looking at it,' said Millie. 'But I thought she was beautiful.'

'Yes, imagine being clever enough to really see people the way Mr da Vinci did. He truly was a genius,' Alice-Miranda added.

'Where are we going next?' Jacinta asked.

Cornelius Trout overheard Jacinta's question and leaned in. 'Some morning tea and then a rehearsal at the Hôtel Ritz, where you'll be giving your final performance.'

'The Ritz!' Sloane exclaimed. 'I've heard that's gorgeous.'

'Oh yes, it is,' said Alice-Miranda. 'Mummy and I stayed there last year when she brought me with her to the shows.'

'What? It's so not fair,' Sloane grouched. 'You've been everywhere, Alice-Miranda.'

Millie shook her head. 'No, she hasn't. She hasn't been camping in our caravan down by the beach.'

'That's true. But maybe you'll take me one day,' said Alice-Miranda.

'Yes, next time we go you can come,' Millie agreed. 'We can play on the beach all day and find pippies and go fishing. I love it down there. You could come too, Sloane and Jacinta, and we could pitch the big tent or sleep out under the stars.'

'I'm in,' Jacinta said.

Alice-Miranda, Millie and Sloane all stopped and stared at her. Sloane's mouth dropped open.

'What? It sounds like fun,' Jacinta replied.

'Seriously? You? Camping?' Sloane still couldn't believe it.

'Why not?' said Jacinta. 'It's not like my mother or father will ever take me. And if it's good enough for Millie and Alice-Miranda, then I don't see why not.'

Alice-Miranda and Millie grinned.

'Well, count me out,' said Sloane. 'The only camping I want to do is under five stars. Like at the Ritz.'

The girls giggled.

Miss Grimm stepped forward and held her arm in the air, signalling for everyone to stop talking and give her their undivided attention. 'Children, I hope you enjoyed the tour as much as I did. Now we will head into the cafe and have a quick bite to eat before we walk to the Hôtel Ritz for a rehearsal. You won't have a run-through for your first performance at the Palace of Versailles at all, so we have to squeeze in these opportunities to practise wherever we can.'

The children were to give three performances on their tour. Their first would be at the Palace of Versailles, to open a show by the well-established Parisian designer Christian Fontaine. Their second was in Notre Dame Cathedral, as part of a mass to celebrate Fashion Week, and the final show was at the Ritz before a parade by the up-and-coming designer Dux LaBelle.

Morning tea was a swift affair, followed by a ten-minute walk from the Louvre to the Ritz, which was located in a very fancy square called the Place Vendôme.

On the way, the children passed another of the banks of bicycles that were located all over the city.

'Hey, professor, why can't we take these?' Figgy asked.

Professor Winterbottom shook his head. 'That's the last thing I'd want to do. Can you imagine trying to control twenty children haring about the city on bikes?'

A little further down the road the boys spotted six tiny electric cars, all plugged in to tall recharging plinths. Apparently they worked on a similar principle to the bikes, with people able to rent them for short periods of time.

Figgy elbowed Rufus as the group waited at a set of traffic lights. 'How cool are these?' He fished about in his pocket.

'What are you looking for?' Rufus asked.

'A card,' Figgy replied.

'But you don't have a credit card.' Rufus looked about to check whether any of the teachers had spotted them.

'No, but I have this.' Figgy produced the swipe card that was the key to his hotel room. 'It's worth a try.'

Rufus watched as Figgy ran the little white card through the machine.

'Hey, I think it's going to work,' he declared as the display began to blink.

Neither of the boys saw the professor approach.

'Give me that, Figworth.' The man reached out and took the card from the boy's hand. 'Thankfully your hotel key will not allow you to rent a car.'

'But sir, we were just kidding,' Rufus protested.

'I can't take my eyes off you two for a minute, can I?' the professor said, shaking his head.

'Can I have my key back?' Figgy grumbled.

'I'll think about it, if you promise not to try to buy anything else with it. Now hurry along.'

The group had reached the Place Vendôme and all its grandeur. The Ritz was located further along, towards the middle of the imposing buildings.

After some lengthy negotiations with the rather forbidding concierge at the desk, Miss Grimm was finally allowed to take the children inside. It seemed the man didn't think much of children and this group clearly didn't fit his ideal of Ritz patrons. The look he gave Harry Lipp was enough to confirm that. Miss Grimm used her best high school French, but Mr Plumpton surprised her by expertly explaining why they were there.

'I didn't know you spoke French, Mr Plumpton,' Miss Reedy said as he returned to the end of the line, where the two had walked together from the Louvre.

'Well, I'm not much good,' he replied, blushing. 'But it's a lovely language.'

Mr Lipp barrelled into the conversation. 'No, Mr Lipp, it's the language of love. I should have gone and had it out with the chap. I did French honours at university. I'd have had him around in a second.'

'Really, Mr Lipp? Then why didn't you?' Miss Reedy challenged.

Alice-Miranda and Millie exchanged knowing glances.

'You could have helped, Alice-Miranda. You're probably the only one who's actually stayed here,' Millie said.

'Just once and the man I remember, who was so kind to Mummy and me, was Monsieur Michel and I didn't see him at all. He worked out the front of the hotel when we were here.'

The children were ushered through the opulent foyer, which resembled a long drawing room, and into an exquisite salon where a group of men were constructing a runway. The sumptuous decorations looked as if they belonged in a palace, not a hotel.

Cornelius Trout had been consulting a very well-dressed woman from the hotel, who was strutting about with a clipboard and looking extremely official. Harry Lipp was busy ushering the children into their positions and working out how much space they would have available for some of their more robust numbers. The rehearsal was set to get underway when, through the open salon doors, Jacinta spotted someone who looked exactly like her mother.

Mr Trout had just started his long introduction on the piano when Jacinta's arm shot into the air.

Harry Lipp tutted. 'Not yet, not yet. Arms by your sides until the bar before we start. I'll count you in. Mr Trout, we'll have that from the top.'

'But Mr Lipp.' Jacinta waved her arm about again.

'What now?' he growled.

'Mr Lipp, I think my mother's out there.' Jacinta pointed towards the door.

'I don't care if Queen Georgiana is out there, young lady, we are in the middle of a rehearsal and you need to focus. As we've talked about many times in the past weeks, no matter if the ceiling caves in or a photographer sticks his camera lens in your face or one of the models falls off her ridiculous high heels, your eyes will be on me the whole time. Am I clear?' he frothed.

Jacinta pouted. She was desperate to know if it really was her mother in the foyer. And if so, what on earth was she doing here and why hadn't she said anything about coming to Paris? Jacinta hoped she wasn't up to her old tricks again – gallivanting all over the place, spending money that she didn't have.

'Focus, children, focus.' Harry Lipp made a 'V' with his forefinger and middle finger and pointed first at the children and then at his own eyes. 'Good, good,' he yelled as the chorus reached a crescendo. His arms rose into the air and the piece ended with a dramatic flourish.

Ophelia Grimm cringed. She couldn't decide what she disliked the most. Cornelius Trout's obsessive hand waving, Harry Lipp's 'look at me' suits or both of them equally. And it seemed that Mr Lipp had been taking some of his conducting cues from Mr Trout too. His gesticulating was wilder than she'd ever seen it. At least the children sounded magnificent. They would no doubt do her and the professor proud. Ophelia glanced at Deidre Winterbottom, who was also frowning.

'Do you think he could tone it down?' she whispered to Miss Grimm.

'Which one?'

The two ladies giggled like schoolgirls before Mr Lipp turned and gave them both his deadliest stare. They were silenced for a moment, until the music began again and they could barely contain themselves. In the end, Miss Grimm and Mrs Winterbottom decided they should leave the room. They held in their chortles until they reached the door and then howled like hyenas on the other side. Before long, Miss Reedy, the professor and Mr Plumpton headed outside too, leaving Mr Lipp and Mr Trout completely perplexed.

As soon as the rehearsal was over, Jacinta dashed to the door, scanning the foyer for any sign of her mother. But if she had been there, she was now gone.

'Do you really think it was her?' Millie asked.

'I'm almost sure it was. No one walks as well on heels as my mother and that woman was like a gazelle,' Jacinta replied.

'Why don't you go and ask someone?' Alice-Miranda suggested.

Jacinta nodded. She walked over to the reception desk, where a pretty young woman with the most perfect blonde chignon leaned over and smiled at her.

'Excuse me, do you have a guest here by the name of Ambrosia Headlington-Bear?' Jacinta said confidently.

'I'll just check for you,' said the woman. She looked down at the computer screen that was discreetly embedded into the countertop.

'*Non,* mademoiselle, there is no one here by that name,' she said kindly.

'*Merci,*' said Jacinta. She walked over to rejoin her friends. 'No, it wasn't her. But I could have sworn . . .'

'Children, well done,' Miss Grimm said as the teachers gathered the group together. It seemed that she and the others had recovered from their fit of giggles. 'We're off to visit the *Tour de Eiffel*.' Miss Grimm was trying hard to perfect her French accent. 'And Sloane, you will be relieved to know that we are taking the bus.'

Sloane nodded to acknowledge the headmistress.

'Is that near the Eiffel Tower?' Rufus asked.

'It *is* the Eiffel Tower,' Figgy replied, punching his friend playfully on the arm.

'Oh,' Rufus mouthed. 'Sure.'

Lucas Nixon raised his hand in the air. 'Excuse me, Miss Grimm, will we be having lunch up there?'

Some of the other children murmured too. They hadn't realized that the rehearsal would go as long as it did and morning tea seemed a distant memory.

'Yes. I've ordered some baguettes and pastries, which we will pick up when we get there. How does that sound?'

'Good, thanks,' he said, smiling.

Jacinta was gazing at Lucas. When he smiled she couldn't help but sigh loudly.

The whole group stared at her.

'What? What did I do?' she asked, puzzled.

'Never mind, Jacinta.' Alice-Miranda reached across and grabbed her hand. 'I don't think you even do it on purpose, you know, but it keeps everyone entertained.'

Chapter 11

After arriving back at the hotel around four o'clock, the teachers were more than ready for a cup of tea and a lie down. Unfortunately for them, the children were still bubbling with energy. Miss Grimm and Professor Winterbottom decided to send them all to their rooms for half an hour's rest. In the meantime the adults would have their tea and decide who would take the children out for a run around in the park at the end of the street.

'Is anyone up for a stroll?' Professor Winterbottom asked the staff, who all lowered their eyes simultaneously. They sipped their tea and hoped that someone else would be the first to volunteer. After an uncomfortably long silence, Livinia Reedy looked up.

'I will,' she said.

'Me too,' Mr Plumpton and Mr Lipp chorused at the exact same moment.

Miss Grimm and Professor Winterbottom frowned at one another. Cornelius Trout looked positively wounded. 'Harry, wouldn't you rather spend some time going over the plans for tomorrow's rehearsals?' he asked.

'No, I think I need some fresh air, my friend,' Mr Lipp replied.

'Thanks for offering, chaps, Miss Reedy,' the professor smiled. 'I'll get on and start looking at the transport arrangements for the rest of the week. I can only imagine the traffic will be chaotic once Fashion Week starts in earnest.'

Mrs Winterbottom felt a tingle on her lips. She tried hard to stifle a grin.

Professor Winterbottom looked at his wife quizzically. 'What's the matter, dear?'

'I never thought I'd hear you use the words "Fashion Week" in such an earnest manner,' she smiled.

'I'd have to agree with you there. I've never had much of a relationship with fashion. I've ignored her completely and she's left me well alone. Unlike you, Mr Lipp. You seem to carry the mantle for all of us fellows.'

The English teacher beamed. 'If you'd like some tips, professor, I'd be more than happy to assist.'

'No Harry, I'll be fine.' The headmaster shook his head firmly.

For the second time that day Ophelia Grimm and Deidre Winterbottom were forced to contain their giggles. They were relieved when Mr Lipp scooted upstairs to round up the children for their games.

In their front room on the fifth floor, Sep Sykes was lying on his bed reading. Lucas Nixon was peering out the window at the townhouses opposite, admiring the French architecture. He scanned the windows. Quite a few had their curtains pulled back, revealing the occupants and their afternoon activities. There was a lady watching television in the townhouse to the right. She was stroking a ginger cat on her lap. An old man was watering pot plants on his tiny balcony a little further down the road to the left and upstairs two small children were in a sitting room playing with some large building blocks.

Lucas saw the curtains move in the window directly opposite. They were open and although he couldn't see anyone, he was certain someone was there. And he suspected that person was watching him.

Lucas turned to his friend. 'Hey Sep, come here.'

'What's the matter?' Sep sat up and shuffled off the bed.

'Can you see anyone – over there?' Lucas pointed at the window.

Sep shook his head.

'The curtains just moved. I think someone's watching us.' Lucas squinted. The afternoon sun was bouncing off the windowpane, creating a dazzling glare.

'I think you're imagining things,' Sep said. He looked down to the street level. 'Although, last night I saw a guy carrying some stuff into the basement over there. He was a bit weird.'

'How do you mean?' Lucas asked as he shielded his eyes against the light and stared at the window.

'I don't know. He just gave me the creeps a bit.'

There was a sharp knock at the boys' door.

'Downstairs in five minutes, lads,' Mr Lipp called from the other side.

'Come on.' Lucas turned away from the window. 'Let's go and see if Prof Winterbottom's got that sports kit. I think I saw a basketball hoop down at the park, so I hope we've got a ball.'

Sep was about to turn around when he saw the curtain move. For just a moment there was a face. It was a young fellow and just as quickly as he appeared, he was gone.

'Hey, you're right, someone is over there,' Sep called to Lucas, but his friend was already halfway down the hall.

Chapter 12

Cecelia Highton-Smith was in a particularly buoyant mood. It was a while since she had spent time alone with her sister. When Charlotte had called and suggested they meet in Paris and have a week together at the shows, she had been absolutely delighted by the prospect. It seemed they were hardly ever in the same place any more. Since Charlotte's marriage earlier in the year to the dashing movie star Lawrence Ridley, it had been even harder to catch up. Cecelia had hoped for a family reunion in New York at the reopening of their department store, Highton's on Fifth, but Lawrence had organized a belated honeymoon at the same time. And while Charlotte still oversaw public relations for the family business, Lawrence's latest movie had taken them to live for an extended period in Los Angeles.

Cecelia hadn't told Alice-Miranda she was coming to Paris yet. She didn't want to get her hopes up in case there was a last-minute change of plans, which there frequently seemed to be. But when the jet touched down at Charles de Gaulle airport, Cecelia felt a flutter of excitement. She and Charlotte could surprise Alice-Miranda by being at the children's first performance. Then perhaps Miss Grimm would give her permission to take her daughter out for a day. There were some designers she was hoping to see during the visit and one in particular, a new fellow that she wanted to sign on.

Of course the family department store, Highton's, had their regular buying team in Paris for the shows, but Cecelia always found that it helped when the boss showed up too.

Charlotte was flying in from Los Angeles and planned to meet Cecelia at the Ritz. She had her own reasons for wanting to see her sister and she was also keen to meet Rosie Hunter, who she'd just employed to report on the fashion shows for the Highton's website and magazine. Charlotte would prefer to have met the woman in person before taking her on, but she seemed to have an incredible knowledge of fashion and a wonderfully witty style of writing, even if Charlotte couldn't find anything she'd published previously. When Rosie offered to get herself to Paris, providing Highton's would pay her accommodation and an amount for each article, Charlotte felt there really wasn't anything to lose.

When Charlotte's plane landed not long after her sister's, she couldn't wait to get into the city. As the car sped along the motorway she rested a protective hand on her stomach. Other than Lawrence she hadn't told anyone her news.

Charlotte's telephone rang in her bag. She fished it out and and saw that it was her husband.

'Hello darling, I'm just on my way into the city now,' Charlotte said. 'Yes, the flight was fine.'

There was a pause as she listened to Lawrence on the other end of the line.

'I miss you too. Of course I'll be careful.' Lawrence was the most attentive husband. She hated leaving him but she was desperate to see Cecelia in person and this week was perfect as he was shooting scenes for his next movie in Colorado for a few days.

'I'll be home before you know it,' she replied. 'Love you, darling.' Charlotte waited for her husband to hang up before she ended the call. As the black limousine pulled up outside the Ritz, Charlotte smiled to herself. She couldn't remember ever being happier.

'Good afternoon, Madame Highton-Smith,' said the splendidly dressed valet as he opened the door. 'Welcome back to the Hôtel Ritz.'

Charlotte stepped out of the vehicle into the warm summer sunshine.

'Thank you, Michel, it's lovely to be here, as always,' she beamed.

The lobby thronged with people. Charlotte walked to the reception desk to check in. She waited while a rather pushy woman made all sorts of unreasonable demands, apparently on behalf of the celebrity she played publicist for. She was so loud that Charlotte was in no doubt about whom she was looking after. When the woman finally stalked off in her six-inch heels, the young staff member sighed in relief.

'Tough day?' Charlotte enquired.

The young woman looked sheepish. 'Oh, no, madame. Not at all. People are just, how you say? Needy.'

'Very, by the looks of that lot.' Charlotte turned and surveyed the ever-increasing entourage milling about in the foyer.

'How may I help you?'

'I'd just like to check in, if I may? Charlotte Highton-Smith.'

'Of course, madame. Your suite is on the top floor. I have a message from Madame Cecelia Highton-Smith who asked me to tell you that she is already in the hotel and is expecting you. Monsieur Michel will have one of the staff attend to your luggage.' The woman handed over the key to the room.

Charlotte looked at the girl's badge. 'Thank you, Claudia.'

'Enjoy your stay, madame,' she smiled at Charlotte.

'*Merci*, and I hope your day improves too,' Charlotte replied. She grimaced as she caught sight of the publicist charging back towards the reception desk. 'Good luck,' she whispered.

Charlotte took the lift to the top floor. She swiped the key and entered the suite, dumping her bag in the bedroom before she walked to the door that led through to her sister's room.

She knocked gently and turned the handle.

'Hello Cee,' she called.

Cecelia emerged from the bathroom. 'Charlotte, darling, it's so good to see you.' The sisters embraced. 'Gosh, I've missed you. Come and sit down. I've ordered tea and champagne. Should be here any minute.'

'Tea, please,' said Charlotte as she sank into the plush sofa.

'So tell me, how are you? How's Lawrence? Are you enjoying LA?' Cecelia fired questions like bullets.

'Good, good and yes, LA is lots of fun,' Charlotte replied.

Cecelia looked at her. 'You're different, Cha. Have you done something to your hair?'

'No, same as always. Perhaps it's the fact that I'm pregnant.' Charlotte beamed.

Cecelia squealed. 'Oh, darling, that's wonderful.' She hugged her sister again and began to sniffle.

'Cee, why are you crying?' Charlotte admonished.

'You know I always cry when I'm happy and this is just the best news,' said Cecelia.

'I'm afraid there's more.' Charlotte took her sister's hands.

'What?' Cecelia looked concerned.

'It's not just one,' Charlotte announced.

'Oh my goodness, you're having twins!' Cecelia gasped. 'Can you imagine how excited Alice-Miranda is going to be? She's always wanted a brother or sister, and you know Hugh and I would have loved that too, but it wasn't to be. Now she's going to be like a mother hen to two little cousins at once. You know, between her and Mummy, they'll have those babies sorted in no time.'

'I hope Lucas is pleased too,' Charlotte said.

'Of course he will be.' Cecelia nodded.

'I just worry. He's had a lot to deal with lately, finding out who his father is for a start, then a new stepmother and now two siblings in one go. It would be a lot for anyone to cope with.'

'I think that young man's far more resilient than anyone gives him credit for. I can't imagine he'll be anything other than thrilled,' Cecelia said firmly.

Chapter 13

'Hello there, Master Sep,' said Monsieur Crabbe. Sep was standing beside Lucas in the hotel foyer, waiting for the rest of the children to join them for their outing to the park.

Madame Crabbe popped her head up over the reception desk. '*Bonjour*, Sep.' Her eyes fixed on Lucas. 'Oh! And you must be Lawrence Ridley's boy. So handsome, just like your father.'

Lucas's ears turned pink. It was fun having a movie star for a father most of the time but some days it was downright embarrassing.

'Did you see my picture?' Madame Crabbe grabbed her framed photograph from the shelf behind her and made her way across the foyer. 'Do you see who that is?'

Lucas looked at the photograph of his father next to a beaming Madame Crabbe. He thought his dad looked a little embarrassed too.

The lift bell rang and a group of children piled out.

'Hey Alice-Miranda, come and say hello to Madame and Monsieur Crabbe,' Sep called.

The tiny child bounced over and Madame Crabbe thrust the picture towards her. 'You must be the little girl whose aunt is married to this handsome man!'

'Yes, my name is Alice-Miranda Highton-Smith-Kennington-Jones and I'm very pleased to meet you, Madame Crabbe, Monsieur Crabbe.' She reached out to shake Madame's hand and then smiled at the man who was still standing behind the reception desk.

'Aren't you just as cute as a button?' The woman grabbed Alice-Miranda's cheek and gave it a squeeze. 'So your aunt is married to my love.'

Alice-Miranda giggled at the picture. 'Yes, I'm afraid so. But I suspect you're not the only woman in the world who's disappointed about that.'

'She is crazy.' Monsieur Crabbe put his hands either side of his head and rolled his forefingers. 'As if a man like him would ever be interested in an old woman like her.'

'Oh!' Madame Crabbe inhaled sharply. She turned and pulled a face at her husband. 'You are so mean. Why shouldn't I be married to a handsome man?' she asked.

'But my darling, you are,' he raised his eyebrows up and down and blew her a kiss.

The children laughed. They hadn't realized there would be entertainment before their outing to the park.

Madame Crabbe ignored her husband and looked at Alice-Miranda and Lucas. 'May I have a picture with you two?'

'Sure,' they agreed.

While Madame Crabbe fussed about having the photo taken, Mr Plumpton and Miss Reedy had joined the children in the foyer and begun a head count. Susannah and Ashima had begged off the walk, complaining of headaches, so there were eighteen children in all.

'Where's Mr Lipp?' Miss Reedy tapped the face of her watch. It was now almost quarter to five and they had planned to leave at least five minutes ago.

Just as she spoke there was an audible gasp as several of the children spotted him. Harry Lipp bounded down the stairs dressed in what looked like an orange velour leisure suit. He had matching orange trainers and a headband in the same bright shade.

'Good grief, what *is* he wearing?' Miss Reedy whispered.

'Looking good, Mr Lipp,' Rufus Pemberley called. He walked over to high-five the teacher, who realized quite late what the lad was doing. He raised his hand just in time to avoid being clobbered.

'Yes, well, one does try to look the part.' Mr Lipp began jogging up and down on the spot.

The group was interrupted by a growling noise and the sound of claws tripping over the tiled floor.

'Lulu, stop right there,' Monsieur Crabbe commanded. The little dog paid no attention. She raced over to Mr Lipp and began to bark noisily.

Monsieur Crabbe rushed after the dog. 'I'm afraid she is upset that I haven't taken her on a long enough walk today,' he apologized. He was wondering if the man's orange leisure suit may also have had something to do with Lulu's distress, but he kept that to himself.

'Oh, she's gorgeous,' said Alice-Miranda as she leaned down to give Lulu a pat.

'Grandpa's got a dog just like her,' Millie said. 'Is she a miniature dachshund?'

Monsieur Crabbe nodded. '*Oui*. Her name is Lulu.'

'Like the hotel,' Alice-Miranda said. Lulu had calmed down and was lapping up the attention as Alice-Miranda rubbed her ears and Millie stroked the top of her head. 'Would you like us to take her to the park, Monsieur Crabbe?'

At the mention of the word park, Lulu began to wag her tail so hard it looked as if it was in danger of being shaken right off the end of her body.

Monsieur Crabbe frowned. 'Oh, I'm not sure.'

Madame Crabbe reappeared, holding a different frame with the new photograph already inside. 'Oh, Henri, please let the children take her. I'm sure they will look after her and bring her back in one piece.'

'Yes, we promise we will, won't we, Millie?' said Alice-Miranda, nodding excitedly.

'Children, we must get going, otherwise your

run around might end up being just a walk there and back,' Miss Reedy said.

Alice-Miranda stared up at Monsieur Crabbe, with her brown eyes as big as saucers.

'Oh, all right, you can take her,' the man relented. 'I will just get her lead.'

Madame Crabbe was way ahead of her husband. 'Here you are.' She handed the green lead over to the girls. There were two plastic bags attached.

'She might, you know . . .' Monsieur Crabbe pointed at the bags.

Alice-Miranda nodded. 'It's all right. We know what to do.'

Monsieur Crabbe picked up Lulu and planted a kiss on the top of her furry head. 'You be good for these little girls.'

'They are going to the park, Henri, not to the moon. I don't get that much attention when I visit my mother for a week,' Madame Crabbe sighed.

'Of course not,' Henri Crabbe said. 'That is because I am always hoping you will stay much longer.'

He then grabbed his wife around the waist and planted a kiss on her cheek.

'See what I have to put up with?' Madame Crabbe laughed.

The children giggled.

'We won't be too long,' said Miss Reedy. She looked wistfully at the couple's display and blushed. 'And I'll keep an eye on Lulu.'

Mr Lipp, who had continued his jogging on the spot, suddenly charged towards the door, with some of the more energetic students hot on his heels. 'All you slowpokes can catch up. Sure you don't want to join me, Plumpy?' he called before he shot out the door.

Josiah Plumpton's nose glowed red and you could almost see the smoke coming out of his little pink ears. 'The cheek of that man. How dare he?'

Miss Reedy touched Mr Plumpton on the arm. 'Please don't let him worry you, Josiah.'

Mr Plumpton frowned. He was wondering how he could compete with Mr Lipp's ever-growing list of talents. Dramatist, conductor and now, apparently, an athlete too.

Alice-Miranda and Millie walked ahead of their teachers, with Lulu guiding the way.

'I don't think Hairy's outfit impressed Miss Reedy at all,' Millie whispered. 'Or his jogging. More pathetic than athletic, I think.'

'Millie! At least he's *trying* to impress her. I think Mr Lipp really likes Miss Reedy. I just hope that she lets him know that Mr Plumpton's her man,' Alice-Miranda replied.

Chapter 14

By the time Alice-Miranda, Millie and their canine guide reached the park, most of the children were already engaged in a vigorous game of basketball, which Mr Lipp was umpiring. Only Sloane was sitting out.

'Do you want to come for a walk with us?' Alice-Miranda called to her.

Sloane nodded. The girls asked Miss Reedy if they could do some exploring. She said it was fine, as long as they stayed inside the park's boundaries.

It wasn't a huge space, but it was clearly well loved, with a basketball court, some play equipment, benches to sit on and pretty flowerbeds. Miss Reedy and Mr Plumpton were soon distracted, discussing the hollyhocks and other flowers growing along the edge of the garden path.

Lulu was doing her best impersonation of a sniffer dog, waddling along with her nose to the ground, until an elderly man leading a stout white bulldog approached. As soon as the little dachshund saw the other dog, she raised her nose into the air and strutted like a model on a catwalk.

The old man dipped his hat to the girls. '*Bonjour*, mademoiselles. *Bonjour*, Lulu.'

'*Bonjour*, monsieur,' the girls said together.

'What a lovely fellow,' Alice-Miranda exclaimed, looking at the bulldog.

He ignored her and barked at Lulu, his tail wagging. Lulu turned her head in the opposite direction.

'Ah, *anglais*? Louis has been in love with Lulu since they were puppies. But she does not love him back. He tries his best but she just ignores him,' the man explained carefully. 'Where is Monsieur Crabbe this afternoon?'

'He's busy at the hotel. He was kind enough to let us take Lulu out for a walk,' Alice-Miranda said.

'You are lucky girls to be left in charge of that dog. Monsieur Crabbe does not usually trust her with anyone. Not even Madame Crabbe. She is like a baby to him,' the man said. 'Enjoy your walk.'

The girls said goodbye and continued along the path.

'So you're not a fan of the bulldog,' said Millie, looking at Lulu. The little dog put her nose even further into the air as if to agree.

'I can see why. He's not the most handsome creature, is he?' Sloane added.

'Looks aren't everything,' Alice-Miranda said.

'No, but if I was a cute dachshund, I wouldn't be falling for an ugly old bulldog either,' said Sloane.

Lulu barked as if to agree.

'Look.' Alice-Miranda pointed at an archway in the middle of a long hedge. 'Do you think there could be more of the park through there?'

'Let's go and see,' Millie said. 'It might be a secret garden.'

On the other side of the hedge, the park narrowed. It was an L shape and ran behind some townhouses. It was another pretty space but didn't look to be as well used as the main part of the park. Lulu sniffed her way along the fence. The girls could just catch glimpses of tiny courtyards at the rear of the buildings. Most of the fencing was made of ornate metal and looked quite old, except for one section. It had thick black fabric running along the inside, completely obscuring the view.

The girls explored all corners of the secret section of the park. Apart from an expanse of lawn and some mature trees, there wasn't much to it.

'Do you want to sit down for a minute?' Alice-Miranda asked as she spied a bench ahead.

'Yes,' Sloane groaned. 'I've still got blisters.'

'Isn't it wonderful to be in Paris?' Alice-Miranda looked around before plonking down onto the seat. 'I just love it here.'

'I can't believe that we're opening shows for Fashion Week – it seems a bit ridiculous really,' said Millie, grinning.

'That's not ridiculous,' Sloane said. 'My mother is soooo jealous.'

'But you said that she hated Paris,' Millie challenged her.

'She does, but she loves fashion. It's killing her that I'll get to see all these amazing shows.'

'Amazing could be one word for them,' Millie said. 'From what I've seen on the TV, weird is more like it.'

'No one says that you have to wear the clothes,' Alice-Miranda giggled. 'I wonder if the models feel silly sometimes.'

'Well, I would, wearing a set of ram's horns on my head, a bathing suit and skyscraper heels,' said Millie.

'No, my mother wears that sort of thing to the supermarket all the time.' Sloane kept a straight face. 'It's what everyone's wearing in Barcelona.'

'Really?' Millie tried to suppress a giggle. 'Well, come to think of it, my mother was wearing a sleeping cat around her shoulders last time I was home. And I'm sure she had some very fetching crab claw boots too.'

The girls' clothing claims became more and more ridiculous and soon they were all laughing so hard there were tears streaming down their cheeks.

Lulu had been sitting under the seat, dozing, when suddenly she began to growl. She scrambled to her feet and rushed out, pushing her nose against the nearby fence. It was the section covered in black fabric. Fortunately, she was still on her lead and could go no further.

'What's the matter, Lulu?' Alice-Miranda walked over to see if she could find the source of the dog's distress. 'Is there a cat teasing you over there?'

Lulu's growling stopped and she began to bark. Her nose was jammed hard against the fabric and no amount of cajoling could tear her away.

Millie and Sloane scurried around to join Alice-Miranda. Millie pushed her face against the fence too and closed one eye, trying to see through the thick black fabric.

'I can't see anything,' Millie observed. 'It's just an empty courtyard.'

Lulu's barking grew louder and more urgent.

'Lulu, please calm down,' Alice-Miranda begged.

The dog stopped momentarily.

'Did you hear something?' Alice-Miranda turned to Millie and Sloane.

'What?' Millie asked.

'I can hear birds and the kids playing basketball,' Sloane said.

'No, it's not that. I don't know exactly.' Alice-Miranda listened again but Lulu started to bark even more fiercely than before.

'Come on,' Millie said. 'We should go.'

Just as the girls turned to leave, a dark shadow

loomed over the top of the fence. A key jangled in a lock and a man burst out of the gate, closing it swiftly behind him.

'*Que faites-vous?* What are you doing?' he snarled.

Millie shot into the air. Sloane wasn't far behind her. Lulu raced forward and began to bark at the man.

'*Bonjour*, monsieur,' Alice-Miranda said as she strained against Lulu's lead. 'Something upset the dog so we were trying to see what it was. Probably just a cat.'

'Take that mutt and get out of here.' The man's eyes narrowed to angry slits. 'Or I will . . . I will call the police.'

'Please, monsieur, we were just taking Lulu for a walk,' Alice-Miranda replied. 'I'm sure there's no need to involve the police.'

Alice-Miranda wondered why he was so irate. It was not as if the girls had been trespassing and Lulu had only been barking for a few minutes at most.

'How dare you?' The man's grey hair seemed to stand on end as if charged with an electric current. 'You need to stop spying on people.'

Lulu's high-pitched woofs were replaced by a low growl.

'Oh, monsieur, I can assure you that we weren't spying at all,' Alice-Miranda explained. 'We don't really look like secret agents, do we?'

The man inched closer to the children. He smelt like smoke and beer.

Millie gulped. She pulled on Alice-Miranda's sleeve. 'Come on, I think we should go,' she whispered. 'Now!'

'Monsieur, I have no idea why you're so cross but it's not terribly friendly, you know,' Alice-Miranda began.

In the distance, Miss Reedy was calling Alice-Miranda's name.

Millie once again tugged at her friend's sleeve. 'We'd better go. Miss Reedy's looking for us.'

'Yeah, come on,' Sloane agreed.

'Your friends, they are much smarter than you are, little one,' said the man, curling his lip. He strode back to the gate, pushed it open and disappeared. The slide of a bolt and the jangling of keys followed.

Lulu rushed forward and barked with all her might.

'Great, turn into a rottweiler now, Lulu.' Millie rolled her eyes at the dog. 'You could have taken a bite out of him a minute ago.'

'Come on, girl,' said Alice-Miranda. She reached down and picked up the little dog, who wasn't going to be distracted easily from her barking. Alice-Miranda had a strange feeling about the angry man.

The children jogged back to the main section of the park. Up ahead, the rest of the group was assembled and it was clear that they were the last to arrive.

'Oh, there you are. I was about to call the police,' said Miss Reedy, looking relieved.

'Not you too,' Sloane snipped. Miss Reedy frowned, puzzled.

'Sorry, Miss Reedy. We were just talking to one of the neighbours,' Alice-Miranda explained.

'Yes, and he already threatened to call the police,' Millie added.

'Why on earth would he say that?' the teacher asked, wondering what the girls had been up to.

'It's all right, Miss Reedy. He was just a cranky old guy,' Sloane said, 'but Alice-Miranda stood up to him.'

'Oh dear, young lady,' said the teacher, smiling at her smallest student. 'I hope you haven't been upsetting the locals.'

Alice-Miranda shook her head. 'Not on purpose. But I don't think the man was very fond of children, or dogs.'

Chapter 15

Charlotte Highton-Smith fiddled with the piece of paper in her hand and wedged the phone between her ear and shoulder.

'Could you take a message, please?' Charlotte said. 'Could you ask her to call me as soon as she gets in. I'd like to arrange a time that we can meet. Today, if possible. Thank you.'

She hung up the phone and frowned. 'Honestly, that woman is harder to find than a comfortable pair of slingbacks.'

Her sister emerged from the bedroom. 'Are you all right?' Cecelia asked.

'Yes, I'm just having trouble getting hold of Rosie Hunter,' Charlotte replied.

'You'll have to tell me more about her. How did you find her in the first place?'

'She found me, actually, and made me an offer that was too good to refuse. She certainly knows her stuff but she seems to have appeared from nowhere,' Charlotte explained.

'And she's going to write about the shows from Paris?' said Cecelia.

'Yes, that's the plan. We'll publish some of the articles in the store magazine too. Her writing is very funny and I think she'll put a much more human spin on some of the ridiculous nonsense that goes on at Fashion Week,' Charlotte replied.

'I'd love to meet her,' Cecelia nodded, 'but not quite as much as I'd like to meet that mysterious Dux LaBelle.'

'Why do you say that?' Charlotte asked.

'I've made an appointment for a preview of the LaBelle collection later in the week but it was very strange. When I said that I was looking forward to meeting Monsieur LaBelle, the fellow on the phone told me that Dux is far too busy to meet clients. I suppose Dux is new and the clothes speak for themselves but if he wants to make it in this town, he's going to have to do at least some of his own PR.'

Dux LaBelle had burst onto the Paris fashion stage a year ago with his first collection of evening wear. His designs were stunning, featuring beadwork and fine lace that were second to none; critics were in awe of his workmanship. His designs had instantly become firm favourites with the celebrity set too. Women loved his work and journalists were desperate to know more about him. But Dux did not give interviews or talk to the press. During his one and only public appearance at his show last year he had worn a mask. It was as if he had come and gone in a puff of smoke.

'I was hoping you were going to sign him up. Actually, I think Ambrosia Headlington-Bear wore one of his gowns to the FFATAS, didn't she? Not that I saw her in person, but there was a lovely shot of her on the cover of *Gloss and Goss*,' said Charlotte.

Cecelia nodded. 'Yes, I saw that too.'

'Well, you might not get to meet Rosie Hunter either at the rate I'm going. She's not answering her telephone at the hotel and I didn't ever get a mobile number for her. I'll try her email.'

Charlotte sat down at the gilded Louis XIV desk in front of her open laptop just as a message arrived in her inbox. 'Oh, here she is now.'

Cecelia picked up a magazine from the coffee table and sank into the overstuffed couch.

'Oh dear,' Charlotte said. 'She says she's just returned from the doctor. She's not well but she doesn't go into any details other than to say that she doesn't want me to catch anything so we should postpone the meeting for a few days.'

Cecelia looked up and said, 'Well, I think she's right. You don't want to risk catching something in your condition.'

'Gosh, Cee, you make it sound like I've got the plague,' said Charlotte, grinning. 'You're right, though. I hope she can still get to some of the shows.'

'Do you want to come with me to see the LaBelle collection?' Cecelia asked.

'Why not? I'm intrigued.'

'Good. That's enough business for now. Would you like some tea? Or a lie down?' Cecelia enquired.

'No, I'd quite like to go for a walk, if you're interested,' Charlotte replied.

'Come on, then.' Cecelia picked up her handbag.

Charlotte retrieved hers and they headed for the lift.

'Where shall we go?' Cecelia enquired as they stepped out of the lift and walked across the elegant foyer.

'What about a stroll along the river? It's such a lovely afternoon. Then we can find somewhere for coffee, or hot chocolate?' Charlotte suggested.

Cecelia was about to reply when she spotted someone familiar. Perched in one of the large armchairs beside a potted fern, and hidden behind an obscenely enormous pair of sunglasses, a well-dressed woman was typing on a laptop.

Cecelia walked towards her. 'Ambrosia, is that you?'

The woman flinched and looked up. She put her laptop aside and pushed her sunglasses onto the top of her head. 'Hello, Cecelia.'

Cecelia leaned in and kissed her on both cheeks, then said, 'You remember my sister, Charlotte?'

'Yes, of course, the beautiful bride. How could I forget?' She smiled and stood to kiss Charlotte's cheeks too.

'Are you here for the shows?' Cecelia enquired.

'Yes, you know what it's like. I thought I'd get in a couple of days before the real chaos begins,' Ambrosia replied. 'See some of the designers. Catch up with everyone.'

'Is Jacinta here with the school group?' Cecelia asked.

'Yes, yes, she is. What about Alice-Miranda?'

Cecelia nodded. 'Mmm, I can't imagine them getting away with leaving her at home. But she has no idea we're here, so if you happen to see them before we do, would you mind keeping it a secret? I want her to get a surprise when we catch them at the first show.'

'Of course. Actually, could you do me a favour and keep my being here between us as well? I have so much to do and I'd hate for Jacinta to be disappointed,' Ambrosia explained.

'But you will see her at the shows, of course?' asked Cecelia carefully. She knew of Ambrosia Headlington-Bear's rather poor reputation for looking after her daughter.

'Yes, of course. I . . . I hope to,' Ambrosia fumbled.

'Well, we should be going. We thought we'd make the most of this glorious sunshine.' Cecelia linked her arm through Charlotte's. 'I'm sure we'll see you again. Perhaps we could have dinner one evening.'

Ambrosia smiled thinly. 'That would be lovely.'

'By the way, have you ever heard of a fashion writer called Rosie Hunter?' Charlotte enquired.

Ambrosia shook her head. 'Why do you ask?'

'I just thought she might have popped up on your radar. Rosie seems to know everything about the industry and yet I can't find a thing about her.'

'If I hear anything I'll let you know,' said Ambrosia.

Charlotte and Cecelia walked out of the hotel and onto the footpath.

Back in the hotel foyer, Ambrosia Headlington-Bear closed her laptop. She packed her things into her oversized tote bag, put her glasses back on and wrapped a silk scarf around her head. She crossed the foyer and scurried down the steps. Ambrosia was glad to have worn her ballet flats for the walk back to her hotel. She should have known that being in Paris during Fashion Week was going to be difficult. But she quite enjoyed a challenge these days.

While Ambrosia missed the glitz and adoration of her life with Neville, her relationship with Jacinta had improved markedly over the last little while. She hoped that Jacinta would be proud of her one day. She rather hoped she could be proud of *herself*, come to think of it. So while she missed Neville, and missed his wallet even more, she had decided that there was no point lamenting life as she had once known it. After all, she'd come from a family of very little means, and now she could go back there and make her own fortune – but this time, she'd do things differently.

Chapter 16

Fabien Bouchard peered through the gap in the curtains. A large group of children tripped along the street, their laughter rising. It was the sound of happiness. Not long before, he had seen a boy looking at him from a window of the hotel across the way. He had wanted to wave but thought better of it.

His mother entered the room

'Fabien, come and look at what I have finished today,' she said. In her hands a black gown sparkled with the glare of thousands of tiny sequins.

Fabien's eyes widened. 'It's spectacular.'

His mother pulled the dress over a naked manne-
quin and unfurled a long train.

'It's your best design yet,' she said proudly.

Fabien turned up the hemline on the dress
and admired the delicate stitching. 'This work is
beautiful.'

Sybilla's mouth twitched into a smile. It was true,
she was an outstanding seamstress.

'Your show will be spectacular,' she beamed.

Fabien paced back to the window. There was
something he'd been thinking about asking her all
afternoon. 'Mama,' he said tentatively. 'Would you
mind if I took a walk?'

'A walk? What are you talking about, Fabien?
You have work to do.'

Fabien flinched. She had seemed so well at the
moment. 'I thought I might go for some crepes and
coffee?'

'There is no need. I have a beautiful new coffee
machine in the kitchen and if you want crepes I will
make them for you.'

Her words were not unexpected but still they
stung. He decided not to press her any further.

Sybilla Bouchard walked over to the drawing

board. 'Your uncle would like one last gown for the finale,' she said. 'What have you come up with today?'

Fabien had been sitting at that desk for hours and nothing had come to him. His mother lifted the drawing sitting atop the pile. Then he remembered what he had been doodling. He rushed towards her.

Sybilla pulled a page of cartoons from under the designs. She stared at her son, aghast.

'This, this is what you have been doing all day? I am working my fingers to the bone and you repay me by drawing . . . what is that? Mickey Mouse?'

Fabien stared at her. 'It's just that I can't think. I need some space, that's why I wanted to go out – to walk in the sunshine and see some people.'

'What people?' Sybilla whispered.

Fabien looked at her. 'Any people, Mama.'

He knew that he shouldn't have asked but he couldn't help himself.

Sybilla closed her eyes. 'There are people out there who will hurt us, Fabien.'

'Mama, please, no one will hurt us.' Fabien walked over and placed his hands on her shoulders.

'There are things you don't know,' she gulped.

'Then tell me, Mama,' he begged.

'No, I cannot. You wouldn't understand.' Sybilla turned and walked away from him.

Fabien gulped. She was acting more strangely than ever.

His mother spun back around and looked at him. 'You have wasted all this time drawing your childish cartoons – when will I have time to finish the sewing if you can't even draw the gowns?'

'Mama, please don't be mad. I made a mistake. I promise that I will work harder,' Fabien said.

'I don't know if that is true. Perhaps you are just like him after all,' his mother hissed. She stormed from the room, slamming the door.

Fabien wondered what had just happened and who she was talking about. *Who* was he like? His father? He didn't even know who he was.

He sat down at the drawing board and screwed up the cartoons that were strewn across it.

Fabien had no idea how long he'd been staring at the blank page when there was a gentle knock at the door.

'Fabien?' a voice called. The doorknob turned and his uncle entered the room. 'Your mother tells me you are stuck.'

Fabien shrugged. 'She is getting worse, I think. I'm worried about her.'

The older man walked towards him. 'I warned you. Asking her permission to go out was not a very smart move, dear boy.'

'But I am so bored, Uncle Claude,' Fabien said. 'Please take me out with you.'

'No, I have business to attend to and you have this collection to finish. We must keep your mother happy, or who knows what she might do.'

Fabien drew in a sharp breath. 'But I didn't mean to upset her,' he began.

'Forget about it. I have something for you.' Claude pulled a photograph from his pocket. Although the detail was blurred, the shape and colour of the gown was clear. 'What do you think of this?'

Fabien took the picture from his hand. 'It's beautiful but what is it?'

'It's old. I thought you might like to use it – for inspiration.'

Fabien hesitated. 'But it's not mine.'

'All fashion is recycled, Fabien. You can use this and make your mama proud, or suffer the consequences.'

'But I cannot pass someone else's work off as

my own.' Fabien shook his head. 'That would be lying.'

'You are so naive. So proud, just like him,' his uncle scoffed.

'Just like who?' Fabien asked, staring at his uncle intently.

'Never mind. Forget it.' Claude turned and stalked from the room.

Fabien threw the photograph onto the desk and walked over to the window. Who were they talking about? He stared into the street for what seemed like an age until the children appeared, returning from their outing. There was a girl walking that little dog that was always with the man from the hotel. There was a boy bouncing a ball and a man wearing a bright orange leisure suit with matching shoes and a headband.

As they passed by, one of the boys looked up. It might have even been the same one who had seen him before. The lad waved. Fabien waved back. He did not care what his mother would say. If the only way to have contact with the outside world was through a window, so be it.

Chapter 17

The children returned to the hotel in high spirits. Jacinta had scored the winning basket for Lucas's team and Mr Lipp let the cat out of the bag that after dinner they were having a movie night complete with choc tops and popcorn. Tomorrow they would do some more sightseeing and there would be a rehearsal before their first performance on Tuesday afternoon. Mr Lipp had promised the teams a rematch too.

Sep glanced up at the building opposite. 'Hey,

there's that guy I saw before,' he said, waving. This time the fellow waved back.

Lucas looked up too. 'We should see if he wants to join us for a game tomorrow afternoon. Even up the teams.'

'He might be a bit old.' Sep squinted, although the glimpse was only fleeting and he really couldn't be sure what age the boy might be.

Mr Lipp held the front door open and the children streamed inside. 'Might I say, you're looking particularly lovely this afternoon, Livinia,' he said with a broad smile at Miss Reedy. 'Paris suits you.'

The English teacher blushed and whispered a barely audible thank you. Mr Plumpton's forehead puckered as he wondered what Mr Lipp had said to her.

Lulu tripped across the tiled floor into reception. Monsieur Crabbe raced out from behind the desk and scooped her into his arms. She licked the side of his face.

'Did you have a good walk, my little one?'

'I think so,' Alice-Miranda answered on the pooch's behalf. 'Although she was upset about something in one of the back gardens. We couldn't see anything. Maybe it was a cat.'

'Lulu does not care for cats. She ignores them,' Monsieur Crabbe declared.

'She doesn't care for that bulldog either,' Millie added.

'Urgh, he is an ugly brute and always trying to, how you say, chat her up,' said Monsieur Crabbe.

The rest of the group disappeared upstairs to get ready for dinner. Miss Reedy said they should be in the hotel restaurant in the basement at six o'clock.

Alice-Miranda and Millie bade farewell to Lulu and Monsieur Crabbe. Sloane had already gone with Jacinta.

'Thank you for taking good care of her,' said Monsieur Crabbe with a wink at the girls.

'It was a pleasure, monsieur,' said Alice-Miranda. Her attention was caught by a small television at the end of the reception desk. It showed a man talking, then the picture changed to a fashion parade before returning to the man. He was waving his hands about and looked very upset.

Alice-Miranda pointed at the television. 'That's the man we saw yesterday. He said that he'd been robbed and the police had just arrived outside the building when we were on our way to Notre Dame. Do you know his name?' she asked Monsieur Crabbe.

'That is Christian Fontaine. He is a very famous designer here in Paris and he is talking about a robbery.'

'Of course! I knew I'd seen him somewhere before. He came to New York for the reopening of Highton's on Fifth. I remember Mummy introduced me to him at the gala.'

'What's been stolen?' Millie asked.

'Fabric,' Monsieur Crabbe replied.

'Fabric?' Millie scoffed. 'That doesn't seem like a very big deal.'

'*Oui*, I would agree with you but it is very expensive fabric called *vigogne*,' said Monsieur Crabbe.

'What's that?' Millie asked.

'Look, there on the screen. It is a beast from South America,' Monsieur Crabbe pointed at a creature bearing a considerable resemblance to a llama.

'I think that must be a vicuña. They look like llamas but they're very rare. That's why their fleece costs so much,' Alice-Miranda answered.

'Mademoiselle is correct,' said Monsieur Crabbe. 'The fleece is worth a fortune and Monsieur Christian had planned to use it for a garment in his collection.'

Millie looked at Alice-Miranda and shook her head. 'A vicuña? Seriously, how would anyone know that?'

'I read about them, I think,' Alice-Miranda replied. 'Anyway, we're singing at Christian Fontaine's show at Versailles. I hope I get to meet him again.'

'There is a reward for the missing goods,' Monsieur Crabbe added as the news story ended. 'It is more than I could spend in a year. That fabric must be worth much more.'

'Poor Monsieur Christian,' said Alice-Miranda. 'It's no wonder he's upset.'

Chapter 18

After a hearty breakfast of croissants, pastries and scrambled eggs, Miss Grimm and Professor Winterbottom outlined the day's activities. They would be taking a boat trip on the River Seine and then visiting Sacre Coeur. Afterwards they would return to the hotel for a rehearsal and then if there was still time, the children could have another trip to the park.

'What's Sacre Cor?' asked Figgy, with a long emphasis on the 'or'.

'It's a basilica,' Professor Winterbottom replied, 'and you pronounce it Sa-cre Ker, not cor.'

'A ba-what-ica?' Figgy replied.

'A church, Figworth. It's a giant white church on the top of a hill.' The professor shook his head.

'Oh,' the lad replied, nodding. 'Cool.'

The professor and Miss Grimm exchanged grins. Figgy was a constant surprise. Who'd have thought the boy might consider an old church to be 'cool'?

Sloane put her hand up and glanced down at her strappy sandals. 'Are we walking there?'

'Yes Sloane, we'll be doing quite a bit of walking, at least to begin with,' the headmistress replied. 'I recommend sensible shoes for everyone.'

Sloane was standing near Miss Reedy and asked if she could dash back upstairs to her room to find her sandshoes. The teacher agreed and whispered that she should make it snappy.

The children set off with the teachers in what was becoming a familiar formation. Professor Winterbottom and Miss Grimm were leading the charge with Mr Grump halfway along the line, then Mr Trout and Mr Plumpton. Bringing up the rear was Mrs Winterbottom and Miss Reedy, who had garnered the attention of Mr Lipp. His simple tan trousers and white shirt were something of a surprise, although he finished the outfit off with a red polka-dotted bow tie and red braces, so still managed to stand out from the crowd.

The group crossed the road just along from the Pont de l'Archevêché, which led over to Notre Dame.

'What's on the bridge there?' Millie called as they reached the intersection.

'It looks like ... padlocks, I think,' Lucas answered.

'Yes, they are,' Miss Reedy nodded. 'They're love padlocks. Each one has the names of a couple in love and the story goes that once the padlocks are locked onto the bridge the two people named will be together for ever.'

'That's a bit stupid,' Sep piped up. 'What if you break up?'

'I think it's a very romantic gesture, don't you Miss Reedy?' Mr Lipp raised his eyebrows at the teacher, whose cheeks looked as if they'd caught alight.

'Me too,' Jacinta agreed. 'I know whose name I'd want beside mine.'

Millie and Sep giggled. Lucas looked ready to crawl under a rock.

'Nonsense, Mr Lipp,' Deidre Winterbottom chimed in. 'It's ridiculous. If you love someone and they love you back, you don't need a padlock to prove it. I can't imagine my Wallace ever buying into rubbish like that.'

Mr Lipp looked stung and was suddenly rather quiet. Jacinta was too.

Millie gave her friend a sympathetic smile and changed the subject. 'Hey, that must be our boat.'

Down below the bridge, several vessels were moored along the edge of the river. Two looked to be restaurants but another had a glass roof, almost like a floating gazebo, and bore the name of a famous French actress, Catherine Deneuve. Miss Grimm and Professor Winterbottom led the group down a steep set of stairs onto the lower concourse. A long line of tourists were already there waiting to embark. The children were directed to the front of the craft, much to the obvious displeasure of several people in the queue. A short man with a shaggy beard snorted and waved his arms about.

'We've been here for ages,' he grouched to his wife, who smiled nervously at the children and told her husband through gritted teeth to stop making a fuss.

Despite the man's protests, it didn't take long to load the boat. With all of the passengers in their seats, it pulled away from the pier and began its slow journey down the river. A commentary blared from the loudspeakers alternating between French and English, outlining information about the grand buildings along the route and then directing passengers to listen to additional information on the personal handsets built into each seat. Alice-Miranda and Millie were sitting in the front row with Jacinta and Sloane. Sep and Lucas were there too. As the boat approached the Pont Neuf, Alice-Miranda glanced up to study the beautiful bridge. A woman was racing along the footpath, hidden behind an enormous pair of sunglasses. Her long black hair was flying.

Millie had been looking at the shoreline and listening to the commentary about the city when she turned to say something to Alice-Miranda.

'What are you staring at?' Millie glanced up at the bridge.

'Nothing.'

'Hey, isn't that –' Millie began.

Alice-Miranda cut her off. 'No, it's not.'

'Not what?' Jacinta turned to see what the girls were talking about.

Alice-Miranda gave Millie a pointed stare and shook her head ever so slightly.

'It's not the Pont Royal, it's the Pont Neuf,' Alice-Miranda replied.

'Seriously? Who cares?' Jacinta frowned. 'It's a bridge. There are loads of them.'

By this time the woman had disappeared and Jacinta was staring at the buildings to the left of the river.

Millie tugged sharply on Alice-Miranda's sleeve. 'I need to go to the toilet.'

Alice-Miranda said 'me too' and the pair of them walked off to another part of the vessel.

'That was Jacinta's mother,' Millie whispered urgently.

'Yes, I know it was,' Alice-Miranda nodded.

'Thanks for stopping me from saying anything.' Millie sighed. 'Why wouldn't she have told Jacinta that she'd be here this week? They've been getting on so much better. Jacinta will be so mad when she finds out.'

'She doesn't have to find out,' Alice-Miranda said. 'I mean, there are thousands of people here this week, in addition to the millions of Parisians who live here. What are the chances that we'll see her again?'

'I hope we don't, for Jacinta's sake,' said Millie.

The two girls made their way back to their seats.

'You took your time,' Jacinta grumbled. 'You've missed lots of things.'

'Never mind,' said Alice-Miranda as she sat down beside Jacinta. 'You can tell us all about it instead.'

Lucas leaned around and looked at his cousin. 'There was this huge medieval palace where they held all the prisoners before they were taken to the guillotine. Imagine that.' He rubbed his neck.

Lucas's face was close to Jacinta's. Her eyes grew rounder and she took a deep breath.

Lucas rolled his eyes. 'What are you doing?'

'Nothing, nothing at all,' Jacinta gulped.

The rest of the children giggled.

Lucas's face turned bright red.

Chapter 19

The students had arrived at the basilica by bus and were allotted forty-five minutes to explore the area. They were split into four groups, with Miss Grimm and Mr Grump taking one, Professor Winterbottom and Mr Lipp another, Mr Trout and Mr Plumpton the third and finally Miss Reedy and Mrs Winterbottom looking after Alice-Miranda, Millie, Sloane, Jacinta and Sep. Lucas had been targeted by Professor Winterbottom, who hoped the young lad might be a steadying influence on Figgy and Rufus, who had become a little rowdy by the end of the boat cruise. He wondered if it was something to do with the fizzy drinks Mr Lipp had bought for the children. Neither the professor nor Miss Grimm had been remotely impressed when Mr Lipp returned from an expedition to purchase water and juice. Instead he carried three trays of fizzy cola and was boasting that he'd saved at least ten euros.

'That's an amazing view,' Millie said. She snapped a picture of her group standing at the lookout below the steps that led to the church.

'It's quite flat for a city, isn't it?' Jacinta said.

'Except this bit,' said Sloane, glancing up at the white edifice atop the hill behind her.

'Mmm, there aren't many skyscrapers when you look out there,' Alice-Miranda agreed. 'It's certainly different from New York. The only places you'd get a view like this are the top of the Empire State Building or the Rockefeller Center. On street level you feel a bit like an ant most of the time.'

'I want to go to New York,' Sloane whined. 'It sounds amazing.'

'It is,' Alice-Miranda agreed. 'I wish you could all meet Lucinda and Ava and Quincy. They're so much fun. Come to think of it, Lucinda wrote to me and said that her father is finally going to bring her and her mother and brothers to Paris. Lucinda and her mother have always wanted to visit but Mr Finkelstein hasn't been a very keen traveller up to now, even in New York.'

'That sounds a bit strange,' Sloane replied. 'Does he have arachnophobia or something?'

Millie giggled and rolled her eyes. 'I think you mean agoraphobia, Sloane, otherwise he's afraid of spiders.'

'Whatever!' Sloane retorted. 'I'm not a diction-ary, you know.'

'No, you're not, but I might buy you one,' Millie teased.

'Please don't fight,' Alice-Miranda begged her friends. 'Anyway, I don't think Mr Finkelstein has agoraphobia. He's just very protective.'

'It would be funny if she was here in Paris now,' Sloane said.

Alice-Miranda wondered. It would be a lovely coincidence, but probably not likely. Lucinda hadn't mentioned any dates in her letter.

'Come along, children, we'd better get inside and have a look before our time's up,' called Mrs Winterbottom. She directed the group up the stairs, where Millie insisted they all pose for several more photographs.

As they entered the church, Alice-Miranda noticed Professor Winterbottom standing in one corner. Nearby was a display of candles for sale, some large but mostly little tea lights. The professor's face was red and he looked as if he was doing his very best not to explode.

Millie had seen him too. She pulled at Alice-Miranda's sleeve. 'What's going on over there?'

'I'm not sure, but it doesn't look good,' said Alice-Miranda.

The girls were reading a plaque about one of the saints when the professor could no longer control his rage. He began to whisper hoarsely. Several of the people sitting in the pews looked up from their prayers, wondering at the source of the noise.

'Figworth, Pemberley, I have a good mind to send you both home on the next flight,' the professor hissed through gritted teeth. 'What were you two thinking?' Unfortunately his plan to have Lucas exert a good influence on the two lads hadn't worked. The professor had been enjoying Lucas's company so much as they walked around appreciating the architecture that he forgot his other charges. But Mr Lipp should have been watching them too.

The professor cast his eyes towards a section of candles where one lonely flame flickered.

Rufus hung his head. 'We didn't know what they were for, sir.'

'And I thought it was dangerous to have so many naked flames in the building,' Figgy added. 'I mean, some lady almost caught on fire when she leaned in to light another one. We thought we were being helpful.'

The two boys didn't dare look at each other.

'That is not true at all,' said the professor furiously. 'I saw you with my own eyes. You were having a competition to see who could blow out the most candles in one breath.' The boys stifled smiles. 'Do not move. I'm going to find Mr Lipp right now. Perhaps he can shed some more light on the situation.'

Figgy and Rufus had to cover their mouths – they couldn't believe the professor had said 'shed some light'.

The professor charged off to locate Mr Lipp, who had bumped into Miss Reedy and was now walking with her.

The professor tapped the Drama teacher sharply on the shoulder. 'Mr Lipp, you were supposed to be keeping an eye on the boys in our group, weren't you?' he hissed.

Mr Lipp spun around. 'Ah, yes, of course professor. Is there a problem?'

'I'll say there is.' He pointed at Figgy and Rufus. 'Those two have been blowing out the candles,' the professor explained as they reached the boys, who were hanging their heads and trying hard not to laugh.

Mr Lipp gulped. He felt as if he was about to be in as much trouble as Figworth and Pemberley. He glared at the two boys.

'It says quite clearly that the candles are lit for prayers. And now they've extinguished at least twenty of them. How much pocket money do you have on you?' the professor demanded.

'Well, I'm not sure.' Mr Lipp reached into his pocket to retrieve his wallet.

'Not you, you twit.' The professor glared at Mr Lipp, who hastily put his money away. He turned to the boys. 'Those candles cost two euros each. You are going to make donations of twenty euros *each* for your ridiculous behaviour.'

The boys stopped giggling and started to feel very sorry for themselves. Figgy hadn't bought his mother a present yet and he'd been looking forward to getting one of those rare action figures from the shop over in St Germain near their hotel. They were expensive too.

'All right, stand there while I re-light the candles. And if you move, I'll be calling your parents.' The professor was almost foaming at the mouth as he took a long taper and proceeded to ignite one candle after another.

An old woman dressed in black from top to toe and with a scarf around her head nodded at the professor with sad eyes. Who knew how many people he was praying for? Clearly his life was heavily burdened, she thought to herself.

Mr Lipp stood next to the boys, wondering if he should assist the professor or just stay well out of the way.

Fifteen minutes later, with the candle situation rectified, the children made their way back to the bus. Figgy and Rufus were in a far more subdued mood than when they had arrived.

'Stupid white church on a hill,' Figgy mumbled as he hopped on the bus. Although he'd spotted the funicular and rather fancied a ride in it down the hill, he'd thought better of asking.

Miss Grimm and Professor Winterbottom decided that there was time for the children to have a return visit to the park and a rematch of their basketball game, except for Figgy and Rufus. The professor had another task in mind for them. There were twenty pairs of school shoes, which the children would be wearing with their school uniforms for their performances, that could do with a polish. Under Mr Lipp's supervision, Figgy and Rufus were the perfect candidates to get it done.

Miss Grimm and Mr Grump said they would take the children to the park and give the rest of the staff some well-earned time off.

Back at the hotel, the children were milling about in the foyer getting ready to leave for the park.

'We're going to be short of players, now that Figgy and Rufus have got themselves into trouble again,' Sep commented to Alice-Miranda and Lucas.

'What about that guy across the road?' Lucas suggested.

'What guy?' Alice-Miranda asked.

'Opposite our window we saw this boy staring at us. He looked kind of sad, and then when we were coming back yesterday he waved – I'm not sure how old he is but he might like a run around outside,' Sep explained. 'I've only ever seen him in the window.'

Miss Grimm arrived and led the group onto the footpath.

'It's that house just there.' Sep pointed at the black door.

'Did you get the sunscreen?' Miss Grimm called when her husband appeared.

'Oh, darn.' The man shook his head. 'You go on ahead, darling, and I'll be along shortly.'

Miss Grimm smiled at her husband and gave him a wave.

Alice-Miranda and Sep were at the back of the line. 'Why don't you ring the bell?' Alice-Miranda asked as they approached the townhouse.

'Shouldn't we check with Miss Grimm?'

'I'm sure she won't mind. We won't be more than a minute,' Alice-Miranda replied as the rest of the group followed the headmistress. 'And you said that he waved at you when we were going home yesterday. It sounds like he's friendly enough.'

Sep gulped. He wasn't sure if they should be approaching strange houses in Paris. But he didn't want Alice-Miranda to think he was a chicken, either.

Sep hung back, so Alice-Miranda scurried up the steps and pressed the buzzer. She waited a few moments and tried again.

'There mustn't be anyone home,' said Sep. He looked up at the window where he'd seen the lad the previous afternoon.

Alice-Miranda shrugged. 'Oh well, at least we tried.'

Just as she turned to leave, the lock snapped and a woman's face appeared around the partially open door. She was very pretty, with piercing green eyes and dark hair pulled back off her face.

'*Bonjour, madame. Je m'appelle* Alice-Miranda Highton-Smith-Kennington-Jones and I'm very pleased to meet you.' The child extended her hand.

The woman looked at her and frowned. Alice-Miranda wondered if she spoke any English at all.

'My friend and I were wondering if the boy who lives here would like to come with us to the park for a game of basketball,' Alice-Miranda explained. She gestured towards Sep, who was standing back on the footpath.

The woman shook her head.

'We're staying just across the road, at the hotel,

and yesterday Sep saw a boy wave to him from the window upstairs so we assumed he lived here.'

'No, mademoiselle.' The woman shook her head.

'But I saw him,' Sep said. 'He waved to me from the window on the fifth floor.'

The woman shook her head again, more definitely than before.

Alice-Miranda nodded. 'Oh well, I am very sorry to have bothered you, madame.'

The woman closed the door.

'Never mind, it was the thought that counted,' Alice-Miranda said.

Sep frowned. He turned and looked up at the window. And just the same as yesterday, he could have sworn he saw the curtain move. 'Look,' he said. 'Look up there.'

For a split second there was a face. And then it was gone.

Alice-Miranda turned. 'I can't see anything.'

'He was there, just now. I promise.' Sep was adamant as he pointed up at the window. 'Fair enough if he didn't want to play with us but why would she lie and say there was no one there? Unless I'm going crazy and seeing things.'

'Or she didn't understand what I was asking,' said Alice-Miranda.

'Why are you two still here?' Aldous Grump called as he walked across the street towards the children.

'We were just meeting the neighbours,' Alice-Miranda told him.

'Of course you were, young lady.' Aldous looked at the tiny child with her cascading chocolate curls and brown eyes as big as saucers. 'And why?'

'Just trying to make friends.'

Aldous Grump smiled. 'Now, that I would believe.'

Alice-Miranda slipped her hand into Mr Grump's and together with Sep they headed for the park.

Chapter 20

Adele's mind was racing. She would never do anything to hurt Christian. He was like a father to her. A very patient father, who coped with all her silly questions and stupid mistakes. But this time she couldn't believe how foolish she had been. When the man had phoned the atelier last week, he had seemed so helpful. She'd thought he was from the company that had supplied the beautiful vicuña fabric.

'*Bonjour*, I am calling from Fil d'Or Fabrics,' he had said. 'Did you receive your shipment today?'

'*Oui*, monsieur,' she'd replied.

'And is it to monsieur's liking?' he'd asked.

'Very much. The fabric is beautiful.'

'And very expensive.'

'*Oui*. I could buy a flat for what it cost,' she said with a laugh.

'And you have stored it properly?'

'Of course, monsieur, it is in the climate-controlled storeroom. Very safe,' she had blathered.

'And that is protected by an alarm?'

'No, monsieur, no alarm, but there is usually someone here.'

'I should hope so,' the man had continued.

'Except when Monsieur Fontaine has dinner with his parents.'

'What a good man! Dinner with his parents. Twice a week?'

'Sometimes three. Always a Wednesday and Sunday and sometimes Thursday too. His Mama is very attentive and she worries a lot about her son. We all do. He works far too hard,' Adele had confided.

'I am glad it has all worked out so well for Monsieur Christian,' the man said. And with that he had hung up.

Now she knew that he had just been fishing for

information. She should have realized. She still didn't know who the man was or how he had got into the building. There was no sign of forced entry.

But it was all her fault that Monsieur Christian had lost the vicuña. She might as well have left a sign out and directions telling the fellow where he could find it.

'Adele,' Christian called from the other side of the room. She did not hear him. 'Adele!'

She flinched and looked up. Her boss was standing between the chief detective and one of the forensic investigators who had dusted the storeroom for fingerprints.

'Come here, Adele,' Christian instructed. He knew that his assistant could be vague at times but in the past few days he had found her incredibly testing.

'Monsieur?' said Adele. She approached the group cautiously.

'There are no fingerprints. Except yours,' he informed her.

'But I . . .' she began.

'Adele, I am not accusing you. Of course your fingerprints will be all over the storeroom. Unless there is something you're not telling us?' said Christian.

Adele shook her head. 'Of course not.'

'Are you sure that you're all right, mademoiselle?' the detective asked.

'Fine, monsieur, just too many late nights getting ready for the show,' she said. 'May I go now?'

'*Oui*,' the detective nodded

'And don't look so worried, Adele. It is a terrible thing and I am dreadfully disappointed that my line is incomplete but of course the vicuña was insured, wasn't it?' Christian asked.

'Of course, monsieur,' she said, smiling tightly.

Bile rose in the back of her throat. She scurried back to her desk and began to move piles of paper about, hoping desperately not to find what she suspected was still there. The little stack of envelopes she had meant to post on the day they discovered the robbery were sitting unsent. And inside one of them was the cheque for the insurance on the vicuña.

She watched as her boss led the two men to the stairs and they disappeared from sight.

Her stomach seemed to be doing backflips and she wondered how she could possibly tell Christian the truth.

The phone rang on her desk.

'*Bonjour*,' Adele answered quietly.

'*Bonjour*, mademoiselle,' the voice on the other end replied.

Adele flinched. It was him. The same man who had asked her all of those questions earlier in the week.

'What do you want?' she demanded.

'Oh, mademoiselle, when we last spoke, you were so kind and helpful. But it seems you are not so happy today.'

'You tricked me,' Adele accused.

His voice turned cold. 'I did no such thing. You have a mouth like a bucket. But now I thought we might be able to help each other. I believe that I have something your boss would like back. Particularly as your lack of security will have voided the insurance anyway.'

Adele wondered if that was true. It hardly mattered, seeing that the cheque was still sitting on her desk.

'I have helped you too much already,' Adele whispered.

'*Au contraire*, mademoiselle. There is something else I need from you. But if you go to the police, I can assure you that Monsieur Christian will never see that fabric again. I've heard that he can ill afford to lose such a large amount of money. Business is tough at the moment,' he said threateningly. 'And you seem to like working for him too. Sadly, not for much longer, I suspect. The other thing you must know is that I can make people disappear. Permanently.'

Adele could hardly breathe.

'What I want is simple. You give me the designs for Christian's next line and I will return the vicuña.'

Her heart was racing. 'But I can't,' she said.

'Then I am afraid that Monsieur Christian will just have to lose all that lovely money. Unless of course you reconsider. It is only a few sketches and no one will ever know. You can tell him they were lost. He is a clever man. He can design another line.'

Adele's hand trembled as she flipped open the notepad on her desk and picked up a pen. 'What must I do?' she wheezed.

The man told her exactly what he wanted and that she should await further instructions regarding where and how they would make the exchange.

Adele hung up the telephone, raced to the toilet and threw up.

Chapter 21

Harry Lipp had slept later than he intended. When he emerged from the lift into the hotel foyer, the rest of the group was already assembled and waiting to head off to the Palace of Versailles for their first performance.

Ophelia Grimm glanced up and flinched.

Mr Lipp's suit was a particularly nasty shade of electric blue, teamed with a multicoloured cravat and blue suede shoes. Clearly he was planning to compete with the palace decor because nobody was going to miss him dressed like that.

Deidre Winterbottom shuffled through the children and found the headmistress.

'Seriously?' she whispered to her friend. 'I wouldn't have believed he could find anything brighter than his red suit, but this one takes the biscuit. I think I need my sunglasses.'

Ophelia Grimm smiled. 'Oh well, I suppose no one could accuse the man of being bland.'

Soon the children and teachers were en route to the palace. They took the train from Notre Dame Station, and Mr Lipp and Mr Trout even contrived an impromptu rehearsal in transit, much to the delight – or annoyance – of the other passengers.

'I'll count you in,' Mr Trout said, and began to click his fingers.

Figgy started a drum solo on the seat in front of him and was quickly greeted with a death stare from the elderly passenger who was being thumped on the back.

'*Ça vous dérange?*' demanded the bald man.

'No, I am *not* crazy,' Figgy protested loudly.

Mr Plumpton leaned over and interpreted for the lad. 'Not "deranged". "*Dérange.*" He asked if you minded. I think he'd prefer you to stop.'

'Oh, sorry. Uh, *désolé*,' Figgy mouthed. He began drumming on his thigh instead.

The gentleman hmphed, but when the lad began to sing the man's eyes almost popped out of his head. It was hard to imagine such a sweet sound coming from the boofy boy. His solo at the beginning of 'Scarborough Fair' was mesmerizing and when the rest of the children joined in there was a brief burst of applause from the other passengers.

The group sang another two songs before Miss Grimm decided that was enough entertainment. She thought a couple of the commuters were beginning to look tetchy and she didn't want to push their luck.

After the excitement of their performance, the children settled back in their seats to watch the countryside whiz by.

'We must be getting close,' said Millie, as she looked out the window. 'We were in the underground for ages and it says here it only takes forty minutes to get there.' She tapped the cover of her trusty guidebook.

'So I suppose *you've* been here before?' Sloane asked Alice-Miranda.

'No, but I've heard it's amazing. Mummy and Daddy have visited and Aunty Gee said that it's awful and ostentatious and she's glad no one in her family ever built anything as revolting.'

'Really? Aunty Gee said that?' Millie frowned. 'Versailles must be really OTT then, because her house at Chesterfield Downs is huge. And I'm sure her other places are even bigger.'

'I suppose so,' said Alice-Miranda. 'I can't wait to see it.'

The train pulled into the station and the children were directed to stay together. Mr Lipp and Mr Trout would go ahead and find out where they were performing. Miss Grimm and Mr Grump led the charge with Professor and Mrs Winterbottom bringing up the rear and Miss Reedy and Mr Plumpton taking care of the middle.

There were hundreds of people heading in the same direction and Miss Reedy was already fearful of losing someone. Her suggestion that they might wear bright orange vests, like some of the other school groups they'd seen around Paris, was met with far less enthusiasm than she had hoped. Miss Grimm had promptly reminded her that the children were opening shows for Fashion Week, not the public transport authority.

The organizers of Fashion Week had taken over

the main palace and hence it was off limits to the general public. But the gardens and other buildings were still open, so the crowds would be as extreme as always. Miss Reedy had arranged that, after their performance, the children would have the opportunity to tour the rest of the palace and gardens, as a reward for their participation. She'd never been to Versailles and, having studied the French Revolution as a young woman, couldn't wait to get inside those gilded gates and see it for herself.

'Wow,' Jacinta gasped as the group rounded the corner and looked towards the imposing palace.

'It's not that big,' Figgy scoffed. 'I was expecting something really huge.'

'I think I would reserve judgement until you see the full scope of the estate, Master Figworth,' Mr Plumpton tutted.

'Have you been before, Mr Plumpton?' Alice-Miranda asked.

'Oh yes, many years ago actually,' said Josiah Plumpton. 'Another of my passions is French history, particularly the Revolution.'

Miss Reedy's ears pricked up.

'Did you hear that, Miss Reedy?' said Millie, as she gave Alice-Miranda a nudge. 'Mr Plumpton is a scholar of the French Revolution. You like history too, don't you?'

Miss Reedy felt the heat rising in her neck. Mr Plumpton looked across at her and smiled. She allowed herself a small smile back in his direction.

As the group walked up the cobblestoned path to the opulent palace gates, Sep and Lucas suddenly disappeared from view. Miss Grimm looked up and charged towards a crowd of men who had surrounded the two lads.

'What are you doing?' she demanded. 'Get away from my boys. They are not buying any of your tacky Eiffel Towers.'

At the sight of the woman flapping like an angry grey goose, the men immediately scattered, plying their trade to other unsuspecting visitors.

Miss Grimm gave the boys a concerned look. 'Are you two all right?'

Lucas nodded. Sep did too and said, 'I thought we could just tell them to leave us alone but they kept trying to put things into our hands.'

'Despicable.' Miss Grimm shook her head. 'I know everyone has to earn a living but intimidating tourists is not my idea of an honest day's work.'

Just as the headmistress finished her declaration,

a police siren wailed towards the palace gates and the hawkers and their wares disappeared into thin air.

'Where are all the celebrities?' Sloane was looking around at the buses parked in rows. 'Surely they don't come by bus?'

'There's another car park over there.' Millie pointed to the far side of the driveway.

'I think most people arrive only just before the show,' said Alice-Miranda. She had attended some of the parades with her mother the year before. 'Anyone really famous seems to turn up a second before things start and then they disappear just as quickly afterwards. I don't remember meeting anyone much because they were all in such a hurry to get to the next event. You know, some of the designers keep the locations a secret right until the last minute because so many people come just to get a glimpse of the stars.'

'Well, I wish someone famous would turn up. How am I supposed to make my mother jealous if no one's here?' Sloane grumbled.

Out of the corner of her eye, Jacinta spied several photographers. She nudged Sloane. 'Looks like the paparazzi have arrived.'

'Thank goodness for that,' Sloane sighed. She immediately stood up taller and flicked her hair back.

Millie was watching her. 'What *are* you doing?'

'Nothing,' Sloane said. 'Just making sure that if I happen to be in shot, I look my best.'

'Sloane, if you haven't noticed, we're wearing our school uniforms. I'm pretty sure that a bunch of schoolkids are of absolutely no interest to the paps,' Millie said with a snort.

'They might be if they knew that Lawrence Ridley's son is part of the group,' Sloane threatened.

Miss Grimm's bionic ears did not let her down. She marched towards Sloane and warned her that if she did any such thing, she'd be on the first plane home again to Spain.

Sloane gulped. Then apologized. She hated the thought of going back to school in Barcelona with that horrible bully Lola.

'Where is this show, anyway?' Lucas asked Mr Plumpton, who was standing beside him.

'I believe that the main event will be in the Hall of Mirrors. Magnificent room. We're very fortunate that Miss Reedy negotiated the private tour for us all later.'

On hearing her name, Miss Reedy looked up. 'It was nothing, Mr Plumpton,' she protested.

'Of course it was, Miss Reedy. Don't give yourself so little credit.'

Millie smiled to herself. It looked like Miss Reedy and Mr Plumpton might not need her friends' help after all.

'Come along, everyone,' called Miss Grimm, waving her hand above her head. 'We have to go this way.'

Ophelia Grimm marched along at the head of the line, cutting a swathe through the gathering crowd. She looked particularly lovely today in a striking black and white dress, although Millie had commented to Alice-Miranda that she thought Miss Grimm's outfit would have looked better with heels rather than the ballet flats she was wearing. And then Millie glanced up and saw that, as if by magic, Miss Grimm's sensible walking shoes had been replaced by a most magnificent pair of black and white stilettos.

'Nice shoes,' Millie said and gave Alice-Miranda a nudge.

'Yes, very,' Alice-Miranda replied.

Chapter 22

Sadly, the choir's first event turned out to be a little less impressive than Mr Lipp and Mr Trout had been expecting. Due to the intense media coverage following the robbery at Christian Fontaine's atelier, tickets for his show were the hottest in town. His assistant Adele had done her best to try to accommodate everyone but the choir just wouldn't fit and they weren't uppermost in Adele's mind either.

Another member of the Fontaine entourage, a rather flamboyant man wearing a spotted kaftan and a red fez, had intervened and directed them down-stairs to one of the palace's huge foyers. He told Mr Lipp that they thought it would be 'cute' to have the little ones in their uniforms greet the guests. But another of the designer's 'people' had decided that the guests should enter the building from a differ-ent point so that they could have a better view of the gardens, hence the children were without an audience.

It was fortunate that neither Miss Grimm nor Professor Winterbottom heard the 'cute' comments as they may have staged a walk-out. As it was, they had to spend several minutes placating Mr Lipp and Mr Trout, who were completely miffed by the snub and ready to take the children back to the city on the very next train.

After a few tears (from Mr Lipp), both gentle-men were convinced that the show must go on. They set about organizing the children into their lines and working out their places. Disappointingly, the grand piano turned out to be a rather small keyboard of dubious tone. It was fortunate for Mr Lipp's publi-cist sister that she had been called away to sort out a drama at another venue, as her brother was furious. She'd no doubt hear all about it later.

Sep noticed his teacher's obvious distress. 'It doesn't matter, Mr Lipp,' the boy said. 'We really didn't know what we were coming to out here and I don't think any of us minds. Do we?' The boy turned to the other children, who all shook their heads and responded with a chorus of 'no's.

'Yes, yes, you're quite right, Sykes.' Mr Lipp pulled himself up straight and smoothed the front of his jacket. 'We'll put on the best darn show we can and if it's just for the portraits on the walls, then so be it.'

'That's the spirit, Mr Lipp,' Figgy shouted, and the rest of the children rallied behind him too.

Harry Lipp's frown lines began to ease and he even managed a tight smile. 'All right, Mr Trout, are you ready?' He looked over at the music teacher, who was standing behind the keyboard like a player in a rock band. Clearly, seating for the instrumentalist wasn't part of the planning.

Mr Trout gave a nod and rested his hands on the keys. He began the introduction and soon enough the children were belting out their repertoire, much to the great delight of their teachers and the security man who had been assigned to monitor the room. No one had any idea where the guests were or what was going on upstairs, but the children were having a wonderful time.

Cecelia and Charlotte Highton-Smith arrived at the palace in plenty of time for the show. They were directed upstairs to their seats in the front row and wondered where the children were. Cecelia was keen to see Alice-Miranda, and Charlotte was practically bursting to tell her and Lucas the good news.

'That's odd,' Cecelia told her sister. 'I thought the choir was opening the show for Christian. I tried to get through this morning to make sure nothing had changed after the robbery but I couldn't get hold of anyone.'

Charlotte looked around at the crowd. 'I can't see Ambrosia Headlington-Bear either.'

'I hope she arrives soon,' said Cecelia seriously. 'It would be a pity for her to miss Jacinta.'

A few minutes later, with the last of the guests being ushered into their seats, the lights dimmed and music blared.

Cecelia leaned towards her sister. 'That's not the children.'

'No, definitely not,' Charlotte replied.

A rail-thin model wearing an extremely short silk check skirt teamed with a white blouse and purple tie strutted down the runway to flashes from numerous cameras. She wore a miniature boater hat atop her blonde hair, which was piled high on her head. Her heels were at least five inches tall; how she managed to stay upright was anyone's guess.

Charlotte and Cecelia settled back to take in the show. They would have to locate the children afterwards. The theme graduated from school girl chic to prom perfection, with the final gown drawing rapturous applause. It was a buttercup yellow evening dress with the most startling lace and diamante-encrusted bodice and a dreamy flowing skirt.

'Pity about the cape,' Charlotte whispered to her sister. 'There was no time to dye the cashmere instead. Apparently Christian is devastated.'

As the beautiful girl strode back to the start of the runway, Christian Fontaine emerged to take her hand and walk the length of the catwalk with her. He stopped at the end and bowed, before turning around and walking swiftly to the other end, where he disappeared behind the curtain.

'Oh dear, poor darling,' Cecelia whispered to Charlotte. 'He looked disappointed, even though the show was as stunning as always.'

'We should try to see him before we find the

children,' said Cecelia Highton-Smith. 'I just can't believe that this has happened to him again.'

'Yes after all that awful business with his wife, it's terribly bad luck,' Charlotte agreed.

The children finished their repertoire. Mr Lipp and Mr Trout took their bows as the small but enthusiastic audience, comprised of their teachers and the security guard, gave a rousing ovation. No one else had seen or heard them at all. Pity, Mr Trout thought to himself, as the children had really outdone themselves.

Outside in the courtyard, it sounded as if someone was upset.

'What do you mean it's closed today? I've come all the way from New York and I am not leaving until I have seen the Hall of Mirrors with my own two eyes.'

Alice-Miranda's ears pricked up. 'I know that voice,' she whispered to Millie.

'No, monsieur, you cannot go in there without a pass to the show,' another voice called.

'What show is that?'

'Monsieur Christian's fashion show,' the second voice replied.

'A fashion show? Are you kidding me? I practically run fashion in New York City. Do you know who I am, young man. My name is . . .' The man barged his way into the foyer.

'Mr Finkelstein!' Alice-Miranda rushed from her position in the first row of the choir and stood in front of the man. He took a moment to register who was speaking to him.

'You!' He looked at her with astonishment and perhaps just a little hint of panic.

'Hello Mr Finkelstein. Yes it's me, Alice-Miranda Highton-Smith-Kennington-Jones,' she replied.

'Yes, yes, I know who you are. But what are you doing here?' Morrie Finkelstein demanded. 'And how come *you're* allowed in the palace?'

'Well, it's quite a long story but we're here,' she said, gesturing at her school friends, 'to sing at some of the shows. Although we've had a much smaller audience for this one than we'd anticipated. Is Lucinda with you?'

'Yes, of course. She's out there with her mother and brothers. I can't believe we've come all this way and the palace is closed today,' Mr Finkelstein snarled. 'And why didn't I get an invitation to this silly show, anyway? My company spends millions on fashion each year.'

Unbeknown to Morrie, his wife Gerda had informed his personal assistant before they left New York that her husband would not be working at all while they were in Paris. Hence the woman had not passed on any invitations to work-related events. When Gerda realized that they would be in town during Fashion Week she had slightly regretted her actions, although she knew that if Morrie ended up at one show he'd feel compelled to attend them all, and this was a family holiday – the first they had ever taken overseas with the children. Besides, until now, her husband had seemed to be having a wonderful time and had hardly even checked his phone messages.

'Perhaps you can come with us?' Alice-Miranda told him. She looked expectantly at Miss Reedy, who had organized the tour. 'Miss Reedy, Miss Grimm, everyone, this is Mr Finkelstein. His daughter Lucinda is a good friend of mine. We met at school in New York.'

Morrie Finkelstein seemed a little overwhelmed by the cacophony of greetings that ensued. 'Yes, yes, I suppose that is true. Alice-Miranda and my daughter are friends.' He frowned slightly and nodded at the tiny child.

'We'd love to have you and your family join us for the tour, Mr Finkelstein. But I'm not sure how long until the show is finished and we can have a look at the Hall of Mirrors. Wasn't that where you said you wanted to go?' Miss Grimm answered on behalf of the group.

Mr Finkelstein looked sheepish. He hadn't actually said that while inside the room.

'I think we should head out into the sunshine for some air,' Miss Grimm suggested. 'Miss Reedy, do you want to go and find out about this tour?'

The children streamed through the double doors into the large courtyard.

'Lucinda!' Alice-Miranda called as she spied her friend standing with her brothers and Mrs Finkelstein.

'Oh my goodness, Alice-Miranda? Is it really you?' Lucinda raced towards the child and the two hugged warmly. 'What are you doing here?'

'I'll explain in a minute. First of all, come and meet my friends.' Alice-Miranda took Lucinda by the hand and led her towards the rest of the group.

Chapter 23

Ambrosia Headlington-Bear had not been the least bit impressed when told that she wouldn't be meeting Dux LaBelle at her private viewing of the LaBelle collection. Apparently he was too busy to see her, and yet, as she had pointed out to the man on the telephone, the only reason he *had* a profile was because she had worn one of his gowns to the FFATAS and her photograph was on the cover of *Gloss and Goss*. She'd only ever seen Dux once, at his show the previous year.

But then, come to think of it, she'd never really

seen him at all. He had worn a mask and his clothes had completely swamped him. At the time she'd thought it wonderfully mysterious but now she just thought it was rather ridiculous.

As the taxi sat idling in the traffic, Ambrosia fished around in her handbag and checked the address. She should have walked. It would have been faster. She looked at the map that the concierge had given her and realized that the street was not far.

Ambrosia tapped the driver on the shoulder. 'Excuse me, I'll get out here.' She pulled a ten euro note from her wallet and handed it over. Then, as she was about to exit the vehicle, she remembered.

'May I have a receipt, please?'

She wasn't used to accounting for her expenses.

Ambrosia consulted her map again and set off. She glanced around at the assortment of townhouses and hotels and decided that every street in Paris looked almost the same. Except for the window boxes. Sometimes they were beautiful and other times full of weeds. But the plants in this street looked well cared for.

Ambrosia reached her destination and rang the bell. Inside the house, she heard footsteps on the timber floor. They seemed to be heading away from the door.

She waited what seemed like an age before finally the door opened. A man greeted her. '*Bonjour*, madame,' he said. 'I am Gilbert and you are?'

'Ambrosia Headlington-Bear,' she said, frowning back at him. 'You were expecting me.'

'*Oui*, of course.'

Ambrosia had anticipated champagne, and perhaps a little small talk about how beautiful she had looked in that LaBelle gown. This man had absolutely no public relations skills whatsoever.

He invited her inside and led the way along the ground floor corridor, where he hastily unlocked a door and pushed it open. The room was large, with bare timber floors and heavily draped windows. He flicked a switch and a dusty chandelier in the middle of the room lit up to reveal half a dozen mannequins. Each was wearing a spectacular gown in shades of fuchsia, black and green.

'Oh my, these are exquisite,' Ambrosia gasped. She walked over to inspect the first gown more closely. The design was like nothing she'd ever seen before and the workmanship was superb. 'Dux is amazing.'

The man nodded but said nothing. Ambrosia had the feeling that this was going to be more of a self-serve viewing. Her French was sorely lacking and this fellow seemed to have very little English either. Ambrosia took out her notebook and began to jot down some descriptions of the gowns.

The man rushed over to her. 'No! No writing. You like it, you buy it.'

'But I was just writing down which of the dresses I prefer,' Ambrosia cooed. 'Of course I'll be wearing LaBelle again very soon – my whole life is one long premiere. I'm sure that we could come to some sort of an arrangement – you know that whatever I wear gets excellent press coverage.'

The man didn't seem to understand what she had said and continued to insist that she put the notebook away.

Ambrosia stared at him. He was a pinched-looking fellow, not at all handsome; in fact quite the contrary.

'I wish I could meet Dux. It would only be for a moment.' Ambrosia batted her long lashes but the man seemed completely immune to her charms.

'No. He is too busy. There is work to be done and he must create. You have to go.'

Ambrosia walked away to examine another of the gowns more closely. 'So, is Dux planning to expand the business at all?' Ambrosia asked. She wasn't really expecting an answer. It was more a question to herself.

'*Oui,* madame. We are, how you say it? Looking for investors.'

Ambrosia spun around. 'Really? That sounds *fabulous.* I'm looking for a project at the moment.'

'Then perhaps, madame, we should talk.' He took her hand into his and raised it gently to his lips. She realized with a little jolt that the middle finger on his right hand was missing.

Ambrosia had met plenty of men like Gilbert before. His oily attempts to be charming were repulsive to say the least, but for now she had to play the game. Ambrosia smiled weakly and nodded.

Of course, she didn't really have any money to invest, but Gilbert didn't need to know that. Ambrosia felt a flutter of excitement. She might just get to meet the talented Dux LaBelle after all.

Chapter 24

'Well, that was disappointing,' Charlotte told Cecelia as they filed out of the Hall of Mirrors. 'I can't believe we didn't get to hear the kids sing. Perhaps we should go to over to their hotel and find Alice-Miranda?'

'Yes, let's,' Cecelia agreed. 'I wonder where they performed and for whom?'

'I'm sure Alice-Miranda will fill us in on all the details,' said Charlotte, with a cheeky smile.

Meanwhile, just around the corner at the top of the garden, Alice-Miranda and the children were waiting to start their tour. Alice-Miranda had introduced Lucinda to her friends and now Lucinda and Millie were engaged in a long conversation about the things Lucinda had already seen in Paris and what else she and her family were planning to enjoy.

'It's beautiful, isn't it?' Millie said.

'It sure is. I still can't believe that we're really here. I never thought it would happen, especially after . . .' Lucinda's voice trailed off.

'It's all right,' Millie smiled. 'Alice-Miranda told me about New York, but it sounds like everything's OK now. And don't worry, I'm sure no one else knows what happened with your father.'

Lucinda smiled tightly. She had been a little nervous ever since seeing Alice-Miranda, and wondered how many of the girl's friends knew exactly how dreadfully her father had behaved. It seemed that he had learned his lesson now: The Paris trip was amazing, and in the past couple of months at home, he'd taken her for frozen hot chocolate, to the top of the Empire State Building and even to the zoo (with a large dose of antihistamines under his belt). He did his park duty and made some unexpected friends in Lou and Harry, two hot dog and pretzel vendors, sometimes disappearing in the afternoons to play chess with them. Her father really had seemed to have changed for the better and she couldn't remember her mother ever being happier.

'We'll be heading into the garden first,' Miss Reedy advised the group. 'Please make sure that you keep up, and don't go wandering off anywhere that you can't see me.'

'Oh no!' Millie grumbled as she rummaged around in her backpack. Her hand shot into the air.

'Yes, Millie,' the teacher said.

'I think I've left my guidebook in the ladies' room.' Millie hoped that no one else had picked it up. It had come in terribly handy so far. 'Can I go and get it? I'll take Lucinda with me.'

Lucinda smiled. The two girls were standing side by side. She'd only just met Millie but it was clear that she was as lovely as Alice-Miranda. Before Miss Reedy had time to allocate another adult to the task, Millie grabbed Lucinda's hand and the two girls darted back through the group and across the large courtyard towards the ladies' loos.

'Miss Reedy, perhaps the rest of us should head into the grounds,' said Professor Winterbottom. He was eyeballing the lads, who had started an impromptu game of rugby with Figgy's hat.

Some of the older girls, Susannah, Ashima, Ivory and Madeline, had wandered off towards one of the souvenir shops.

'Yes, that sounds like a good idea,' the English teacher said. 'Come along, everyone,' she called, while the other adults rounded up the students and followed her towards the gatehouse where the tickets would be collected.

'I'll wait here for Millie and Lucinda,' Mrs Winterbottom offered. 'We'll see you on the other side.'

Miss Reedy nodded.

As the children walked through the garden entrance, there was a collective gasp.

'Cool!' Figgy exclaimed, turning his head left and right to take in the astonishing view. 'Is this for real?'

'I warned you not to speak too soon,' Mr Plumpton said as he nudged the lad.

Laid out before them, the gardens of Versailles stretched on almost as far as the eye could see.

Meanwhile, back in the ladies' room, Millie had located her book exactly where she'd left it on the end of the countertop. Both girls decided they should take the opportunity to use the facilities and popped into two toilet stalls side by side. There was an echo of footsteps on the tiles and the sound of a hushed voice.

'Why must I speak to you in English?' the woman asked.

There was a pause.

'But I didn't. You tricked me.'

Lucinda flushed the toilet and walked out of the stall. Millie followed. It was a young woman speaking. Her face was red and her eyes puffy. She wore very stylish clothes and extremely high heels.

'I cannot speak now,' the young woman whispered.

Millie and Lucinda walked out into the courtyard, where Mrs Winterbottom was waiting for them.

'Ready?' the older woman asked.

The girls nodded, but lagged behind her.

'I saw that girl earlier, in the courtyard,' Lucinda whispered. 'She was on the phone then too and she was trembling. She told someone that they could have the designs and then she hung up as soon as she realized I was standing nearby.'

'That's weird. I think I've seen her before too.' Millie pondered for a moment. 'Ah, that's it! She must work for Monsieur Fontaine. When we arrived in Paris, we saw some police cars speeding down a street near Notre Dame and then a man rushed out and said that he'd been robbed. That girl was with him. We didn't know he was Christian Fontaine at the time but it's been all over the news since then. Of course she's here because of the show.'

'I wonder what she was talking about then,' Lucinda said.

'She sounded scared. Do you think it could have had something to do with the robbery?' Millie asked. 'Maybe we should tell someone.'

'I don't know. We haven't got any proof of anything. But she was upset about something, that's for sure,' Lucinda said.

Millie nodded. She was having a strange feeling about that girl. She would tell Alice-Miranda about it as soon as she could.

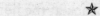

Alice-Miranda had been thrilled to learn that the Finkelsteins were staying just around the corner from l'Hôtel Lulu. The choir's next performance wasn't until the following evening, so she had asked

Miss Grimm if Lucinda could join them for their free day. Miss Grimm agreed, as long as her parents approved. She'd had a very enjoyable wander around the gardens with Gerda Finkelstein, and Morrie Finkelstein had been completely charming.

When Alice-Miranda and Lucinda went together to seek Mr Finkelstein's permission, he was reluctant.

'I'm not sure about this. We're in a foreign country, Lucinda, and I just don't think that it's safe,' Morrie had responded with a deep frown.

Gerda stepped in immediately. 'Oh for heaven's sake, Morrie Finkelstein. Alice-Miranda has taken better care of our daughter than you at times, so of course she can go. And then you can take me to the Eiffel Tower for lunch. It would be nice to have some romance in my life. Even if it is with you.'

Lucinda and Alice-Miranda laughed. Miss Grimm and Mrs Finkelstein would make the arrangements and the girls would meet in the morning.

The children arrived back at the hotel exhausted after their day at Versailles. They stayed far longer than Miss Grimm had originally planned because Figgy disappeared in Marie Antoinette's bedroom. He had taken a detour through a secret door and couldn't find his way back out again. Palace security had found him sobbing in the basement an hour after the professor noticed he was missing.

'*Bonjour*, children,' called Monsieur Crabbe as the group trooped through the foyer.

'*Bonjour*, monsieur,' the chorus echoed back.

Lulu raced out from behind the reception desk, eager for some attention.

'She has missed you all today.'

Alice-Miranda and Millie knelt down to give the tiny dog a scratch. She immediately rolled onto her back so they could rub her belly.

Madame Crabbe appeared from the office. '*Bonjour.* How was your visit to the chateau?'

Millie was the first to answer. 'It was amazing! Well, the palace and grounds were, not so much the performance.'

Madame Crabbe frowned. 'It was not good?'

'We thought we were pretty good, it's just that we didn't really have an audience,' Alice-Miranda explained.

'What a shame,' Madame said. 'It is plain silly to have no one to hear you.'

'We thought so too,' Sep chimed in, 'but surely there will be people in the cathedral, even if it's just the tourists. And we've already rehearsed at the Ritz so we know that we'll have an audience there.'

'I will come and watch you at Notre Dame,' said Madame Crabbe.

'And tonight when you come back from your evening meal, you will have a special treat,' Monsieur Crabbe said with a wink.

'What's that?' Alice-Miranda asked.

'I am going to play my accordion for you,' the man replied.

Madame Crabbe groaned. 'Urgh, that is not a treat, that is torture.'

'It's all arranged. Monsieur Trout, he and I will be the evening entertainment.' Monsieur Crabbe gave a mock bow.

'I am going out,' Madame Crabbe said. 'No offence to Mr Trout. I am sure he is a wonderful performer, but I hate the accordion.'

The children laughed.

'All right, you lot. Upstairs for a rest before we head out for dinner in half an hour,' Professor Winterbottom commanded. 'And we'll look forward to that concert later on.'

The group disappeared but Alice-Miranda waited behind.

Alice-Miranda pulled a newspaper from her

backpack. 'Monsieur Crabbe? Do you remember the other night we talked about Monsieur Christian and the stolen fabric?'

'*Oui*. Of course. A very bad business,' he replied.

'Well, I picked this up on the train this afternoon.' She placed the paper on the bench in front of him and stood up on her tippy toes.

Under the headline was a photo of Christian Fontaine and a smaller photo of a woman. She had long straight hair and was very thin and pretty.

Monsieur Crabbe scanned the page. 'That woman was married to Monsieur Fontaine but she disappeared many years ago after he caught her stealing. Although it was never proven in court – this article says that there is still a warrant out for her arrest. It was a terrible scandal. They had been like pin-ups for love. Their photographs were all over the place and their business was very famous. It did not make any sense at all. He says that it is the same thing happening all over again.'

Alice-Miranda frowned. 'Does it say what she stole?'

'Yes, she was selling his designs and fabric to people who were making copies,' Monsieur Crabbe replied.

'I wish we'd been able to meet Monsieur Christian today but we didn't even see him. He looks so sad in that picture.'

'It is not for you to worry about, little one. The police are working on the case.'

'Of course,' Alice-Miranda nodded and looked at the photographs again. 'It's just that she looks sort of familiar.'

'Really? Can you think why?' the man asked.

Alice-Miranda shook her head. 'No, it's just something about her.'

'Well, if you remember, you must tell me and we can alert the police,' Monsieur Crabbe said. Alice-Miranda waved goodbye to the man and raced upstairs. Something about those pictures niggled at her. She had a strange feeling about that woman she simply couldn't shake.

Chapter 25

'My crepes were delicious,' Alice-Miranda remarked as she bounded along beside Sep on their way back to the hotel that evening. 'Chicken and mushroom is almost as good as lemon and sugar.'

'Nutella is still my favourite,' the boy replied. 'I think I might move to Paris. Chocolate crepes three times a day sounds perfect to me.'

The group formed a long line, with Miss Grimm in the lead and Professor Winterbottom bringing up the rear. They were spread out for quite a distance, snaking all the way back to the restaurant. As Alice-Miranda and Sep rounded the corner into their street he noticed the man he'd seen earlier in the week, standing out the front of the townhouses.

Millie had caught up and was walking beside the pair. She noticed the man too. 'Hey, isn't that the guy who told us off when we were at the park the other afternoon?'

Alice-Miranda looked. 'Yes, I think so. Perhaps he'll be in a better mood this evening.'

'I doubt it. He was horrible,' said Millie. 'He certainly didn't like children or dogs. Not one little bit.'

Sep glanced at the girls. 'What do you mean he told you off?'

'You know, the first day we were at the park. We took Lulu for a walk and there was a secret part to the garden. All of a sudden Lulu started growling and barking and then that man came through a gate and told us to get lost,' Millie explained.

'I saw him the first night we were here. He was carrying long rolls of something out of a car and into the basement of that townhouse there.' Sep pointed at the place with the black door. 'That's right! Before that he was having a pretty big argument with someone over the phone. It was mostly in French but then I remember he said something about a chinchilla – I thought it was a weird thing to say.'

As the children drew closer, Alice-Miranda called '*Bonjour*, monsieur.'

'*Bonjour*, mademoiselle.' The man nodded at her and dipped his cap but his expression remained stony.

After the trio had passed him, Alice-Miranda whispered, 'We must have caught him on a bad day before.'

'I suppose so, but he wasn't exactly friendly just then,' Millie replied.

Alice-Miranda was thinking. She turned to Sep. 'Do you remember if he said anything else in English?'

'No,' Sep replied. 'He was across the road and he was speaking French most of the time. Why?'

'No reason,' Alice-Miranda said. But her mind was ticking. She thought about Monsieur Fontaine's story in the newspaper. It did seem like a very strange coincidence that the man would be so upset about a small South American rodent.

'And he took the rolls into the basement of that house there?' Alice-Miranda pointed.

Sep nodded. 'Who are you? Inspector Clouseau?'

Alice-Miranda shook her head. Suddenly she turned and ran back towards the man.

'Alice-Miranda, what are you doing?' Millie called after her.

She reached the fellow and stopped.

'*Bonjour*, monsieur,' Alice-Miranda said again. She studied his pointy face.

'*Bonjour*,' the man replied. His brow wrinkled slightly as he pondered the reason for her return.

'My name is Alice-Miranda Highton-Smith-Kennington-Jones.' She held out her hand.

The man looked at her for a moment but did not respond.

'Monsieur?' she asked. 'Do you have a name?'

'Of course,' he said, but didn't offer it.

'Monsieur,' she began, 'my friends and I are staying just over there at l'Hôtel Lulu. It's a lovely place and Monsieur and Madame Crabbe are wonderful hosts. We met the other afternoon. Do you remember?'

He glanced at her face, shrugged and then looked away into the distance.

'We were in the park and we had Monsieur Crabbe's little dog, who is also called Lulu, with us.

She was rather upset about something and you came out through a gate,' Alice-Miranda reminded him. She wondered if he really couldn't remember or if he was just avoiding the conversation.

'Ah, *oui*. The barking dog. I was, how you say it? Not happy. I had a headache and your dog was causing me pain,' the man said matter-of-factly.

Alice-Miranda frowned. 'Oh, I am sorry. We didn't mean to upset you,' she said. 'I'm glad you didn't call the police.'

The man cleared his throat. 'I wasn't really going to call the police,' he said.

'I am glad about that,' Alice-Miranda replied. 'I'm sure the police are far too busy dealing with real criminals.'

'What criminals?' he asked.

'Well, whoever has stolen that expensive fabric from Monsieur Christian, for example,' said Alice-Miranda. She watched his face closely.

'What fabric?' His voice was rock-steady.

'The vicuña. But it sounds like the police have some good leads. I've heard that the police think Monsieur Christian's ex-wife is part of it. Well, it's nice to see you again, monsieur.'

The man simply nodded, then walked down the steps into the basement.

Alice-Miranda stared at the door. She must have got it wrong, she thought. The man hadn't been feeling well, that's all. But as she ran back towards her friends she had a strange feeling that there was more to him than met the eye.

'What did he say?' Millie asked.

'He said that he had a headache when we saw him in the park. That's why he was so upset,' Alice-Miranda replied.

'You don't look convinced,' said Sep.

Alice-Miranda tried to shake off her strange feeling. 'I'm sure it's nothing,' she said. 'Come on, we don't want to miss out on Monsieur Crabbe and Mr Trout's musical extravaganza, do we?'

'Really?' Millie rolled her eyes. 'I think we do.'

Alice-Miranda grabbed her friend's hand and they ran along the footpath with Sep close behind.

Millie was sure that there was something Alice-Miranda wasn't telling them. She would have to find out later.

Chapter 26

Charlotte Highton-Smith sat at the computer scanning the contents of her mail. Her sister was sipping a cup of tea and reading the morning newspaper on the sofa behind her.

Charlotte giggled.

'What are you laughing at?' Cecelia looked up and asked.

'Rosie Hunter's first article. It's a general overview of what happens at Fashion Week – you know, the chaos and things celebrities will do to get the best positions at the shows. She was reminding me of that hideous woman at reception yesterday. When I checked in she was demanding that her mistress's bath be filled with goat's milk warmed to 44 degrees. I thought I was hearing things but no, that was the request.'

'Who are these people?' Cecelia giggled. 'That's a new one. But do you remember the first year Mummy and Daddy brought us to the shows and that ghastly pop star had her ridiculous hat fashioned from a full-sized ironing board. She had people diving for cover every time she turned around.'

'And didn't she have a pet rabbit in her handbag, too? I can't imagine how it just sat there. Probably loved the entertainment, actually,' Charlotte added.

'It sounds like you're happy with Rosie's first effort, then?' Cecelia quizzed.

'Oh, yes. I'm disappointed she didn't make it to Versailles yesterday for Christian's show. But I think this article will make a splash and then hopefully she'll be feeling better and can get out to cover more things.'

'Poor woman can't help being unwell, Cha,' Cecelia said, 'and it sounds as if she's keen to impress.'

Charlotte stared at the screen. She read the last few lines of Rosie's email and then read them again.

'So are you OK if we leave in about half an hour? We can take a taxi over to the children's hotel in St Germain and then we can walk from there,' Cecelia said.

Charlotte didn't respond. She was still engrossed in whatever was on the screen.

'Charlotte, did you hear what I said?' Cecelia asked a little louder.

'Sorry, Cee, I was just reading something that Rosie had written in her email. She's left me a bit of a teaser.'

'What is it?' Cecelia asked.

'She hasn't said much, just that if things unravel the way she's expecting them to, we'll have a huge scoop,' Charlotte explained.

'I wonder what she means by that? A huge collection, a huge frock, a huge designer? I hope the woman's not trying to be too clever. I guess you'll just have to wait and see,' said Cecelia. 'Now are you sure about today?'

Cecelia Highton-Smith had arranged with Miss Grimm to take Alice-Miranda and Lucas out. The headmistress had scheduled a quiet day – the group might venture to the park or on a short walk but she didn't want the children to be too tired before their performance at the mass at Notre Dame that evening. Cecelia had been very surprised to learn too that the Finkelsteins were in town. She was thrilled when Morrie gave his permission for Lucinda to join their outing. Sep, Sloane, Jacinta and Millie were coming along too, so in all they would be looking after seven children.

'Oh yes, I can't wait to see the kids. But you haven't said where we're going yet,' her sister replied.

'Somewhere Mummy and Daddy used to take us when we were girls. You always loved it,' Cecelia said mysteriously.

'OK, if you say so.' Charlotte hit send. She had replied to Rosie that she loved the article and it would be posted on the Highton's website immediately. As for the other teaser, she didn't comment. Better not to engage with the woman on that until there was something to comment about.

Chapter 27

The children were gathered in the dining room for their breakfast when Miss Grimm pulled Alice-Miranda aside. She ushered her upstairs into the hotel foyer.

'I know that you were looking forward to spending the day with Lucinda but I'm afraid there's been a change of plans,' the headmistress informed her.

'Really? Did Mr Finkelstein change his mind?' Alice-Miranda asked. 'I'm sure I could call and convince him that Lucinda will be perfectly safe with us for the day. I mean, you're a headmistress and we also have a headmaster with the group too and everyone knows you have to be more responsible than almost anyone in the world. Except perhaps someone like Mr Grayson, who looks after a whole country.' Alice-Miranda was referring to the President of the United States, whom she had met at her aunt's wedding earlier in the year.

'Oh, you're very kind, young lady, but I'm afraid things have changed,' Miss Grimm said with a frown. The headmistress was facing the hotel entrance and had just seen Alice-Miranda's mother enter.

'I hope you're not too disappointed, darling,' Cecelia Highton-Smith added.

Alice-Miranda spun around. 'Mummy!'

Cecelia scooped the tiny child into her arms. Charlotte walked through the door just as Alice-Miranda's feet touched the floor again.

'Aunt Charlotte,' she cried and raced towards her favourite aunt. Charlotte leaned down to hug the child. She then kissed her on both cheeks, on the tip of her nose and on her forehead, just as they always did. It was their own special greeting.

Alice-Miranda frowned. 'Am I too heavy now that I'm eight?' she asked, referring to the fact that Charlotte usually picked her up and twirled her in her arms.

'Oh, darling.' Charlotte smiled. 'It's not that at all. I just have to be a little bit careful at the moment.'

'Did you hurt yourself?' Alice-Miranda stepped back and looked at her beloved aunt.

'No, nothing like that. But where's Lucas? I'd like to talk to you both.'

Miss Grimm was way ahead of her and had already gone downstairs to get the lad.

He walked into the foyer and was stunned to see his stepmother and her sister.

'Charlotte, what are you doing here?' Lucas hurried over and gave her a hug.

'Hello, handsome. Cecelia and I thought we'd surprise the two of you. We went to a show yesterday expecting to see some fabulous new singing group who were supposed to be performing but they didn't turn up,' Charlotte teased. 'It was at the Palace of Versailles, too. Imagine that!'

'We were there. They moved us to this out-of-the-way place and nobody saw us,' Lucas protested. 'But what are you doing in Paris? Is Dad here too?'

'Cee and I decided to spend the week together and see some of the shows. And of course your shows too – if you ever bother to turn up.' Charlotte winked. 'And no, your father is in the wilds of Colorado shooting scenes for the movie.'

Madame Crabbe was watching the scene play out from the reception desk. She was trying to keep quiet but could no longer contain herself. She practically burst through the reception counter as she scurried over to Charlotte.

'Excuse me, madame,' she said, 'I couldn't help hearing. Are you married to this man?' She was holding the photograph of her and Lawrence Ridley.

Charlotte studied the picture. It was her husband all right. And the woman in front of her.

'*Oui*, madame,' Charlotte said kindly. She thought Lawrence looked a little overwhelmed but she wasn't about to say so.

'You are a beautiful woman. And if he can't have me then he deserves someone as beautiful as you. And your children, they are beautiful too.' Mrs Crabbe glanced at Alice-Miranda and Lucas, who both grinned.

'Thank you,' Charlotte giggled. 'I see you've met Lawrence.'

'*Oui*. He is a gentleman and I adore his movies.'

'Tell her the truth, wife,' shouted Monsieur Crabbe, who was watching the interaction from behind the desk. 'You adore her husband full stop, amen. But I have told her that a handsome man like Monsieur Ridley will not be interested in an old woman like her.'

'Monsieur Crabbe, that's horrible,' Alice-Miranda scolded. 'Madame Crabbe is lovely and young and she's very beautiful. You are lucky to have her. And she's lucky to have you too, of course.'

'*Merci*, Alice-Miranda. You see what I have to put up with,' Madame Crabbe tutted, and shook her head. 'It is a pleasure to meet you, madame.' She took Charlotte's hand in hers and drew in a sharp breath. 'You and Monsieur Ridley will have a beautiful baby too.'

Charlotte's eyes widened.

'How did you know?' she looked at Madame Crabbe.

The woman shrugged. 'Just a feeling, but it seems I was right.'

'What baby?' Lucas asked.

Alice-Miranda beamed. 'That's why you didn't pick me up. You're having a baby!'

Charlotte looked at Lucas and Alice-Miranda and nodded.

'That's fantastic!' Lucas exclaimed. 'I'm going to be a big brother.'

'And I'm going to be a big cousin,' Alice-Miranda added.

'Well, there's a little bit more to it than that,' Charlotte gulped. 'You see, Lawrence and I are having . . .' She held up two fingers and whispered, 'twins.'

Alice-Miranda and Lucas looked at each other, their mouths gaping open.

Lucas finally found his voice. 'Two?'

Charlotte nodded. Cecelia was standing beside her sister, watching the children's reactions.

'That's awesome!' Lucas reached out and hugged his stepmother, then released her quickly. 'Oh, sorry, I didn't hurt you, did I? Sorry, little guys,' he said, staring at Charlotte's middle.

Charlotte shook her head. 'I think these babies are going to be tougher than you think.' A tear wobbled in the corner of her eye. 'I know your father wanted to be here to tell you too, Lucas, but he'll be so thrilled that you're happy.'

Lucas looked surprised. 'Of course I'm happy. I've always wanted a brother or sister. I just wanted to know who my dad was to start with, and now I have all of you. It's unreal!'

'Your father *is* here, Monsieur Lucas.' Madame Crabbe held up the photograph of her and Lawrence. 'And he is smiling . . . all the time.'

Everyone laughed.

Alice-Miranda hugged her cousin. 'It's going to be great, Lucas,' she said as she stepped back. 'We'll be able to look after the babies and give them their bottles and change their nappies.'

He wrinkled his nose. 'You can take care of the nappies, little cousin.'

Miss Grimm congratulated Charlotte, as did Madame and Monsieur Crabbe.

Cecelia caught her daughter's eye. 'Well, darling, did Miss Grimm tell you that we're spending the day together?'

Alice-Miranda shook her head.

'I thought she might like a surprise,' said Miss Grimm. 'I'll just go and get the others.'

'Which others?' Alice-Miranda asked.

'It hardly seemed fair that we would take you and Lucas on your own, so I've arranged with Miss Grimm and Professor Winterbottom to take Millie and Sloane and Sep and then we'll head over to get Lucinda, too. I don't think I could manage the rest of the group,' her mother explained.

'Oh, that sounds wonderful,' Alice-Miranda beamed. 'What are we going to do?'

Charlotte smiled and said, 'Your mother hasn't even told me what she's got planned. She's been very mysterious.'

The other children arrived in the foyer.

'Can we tell them the news?' Lucas whispered in his stepmother's ear.

She nodded. 'But only if they promise not to tell anyone. I couldn't stand having the paparazzi staking out the house for the next five months.'

Lucas tugged on his cousin's shirt. 'Let's tell them later,' he said, nodding at the other kids. 'I think I want this to be our secret just for a little while.'

Alice-Miranda agreed.

Chapter 28

Fabien Bouchard's eyelids felt like lead weights. The golden glow around the edge of the curtains told him how long he had worked. Now all he wanted was to climb into bed and sleep, at least for a few hours. But his mother would be up soon.

He had worked through the night to finish the last design for the collection. He had discarded many sketches but finally he had his gown.

The door handle turned and Sybilla Bouchard entered the room, carrying a tray with tea and toast.

She looked at the bed in the middle of the room and gasped. It had not been slept in.

'Fabien?' she called urgently. 'Where are you?' Her heart hammered inside her chest and she had to catch her breath.

He had drifted off to sleep again at the drawing board. 'My son,' she exhaled loudly as she saw the lad with his head resting on the angled board. She looked at his profile and touched him gently on the cheek.

Fabien jolted awake. He sat up and yawned widely.

His mother's eyes fell to the sketch on the board. 'This is beautiful. It reminds me of . . .'

'Of what, Mama?' Fabien asked.

'Nothing. You have worked hard and I am pleased. That's all that matters.'

She pushed the papers around on the drawing board, looking at the half-finished sketches.

'These are good too,' she said. 'But you are tired. I'm afraid I will be working all day to get this done, so sleep and read, my darling, and I will be back this evening with your supper. There is food in the kitchen for your lunch.'

'Is Uncle Claude home?' he asked.

'No.' She shook her head. 'Your uncle has important business. But we had breakfast together this morning before he left.'

Sybilla leaned down to kiss Fabien's cheek. 'Your uncle will be so proud.'

And with that she left the room. Fabien stood up from his desk and stretched. He remembered that he was still wearing the same clothes he had on the day before, so he showered quickly and found some fresh trousers and a shirt.

He ate his breakfast and flicked through one of his old sketchpads. It didn't take long before he was restless. He wandered to the window and saw a group of children from the hotel across the street. They were standing by the door, with two women hovering. One of the boys looked up towards him. He smiled. Fabien raced downstairs and opened the front door. He snibbed the lock so he could get back in later. He watched them from there until they reached the end of the street and turned left. Then he did something he'd never done before. He pulled the door closed and headed out after them.

Chapter 29

Alice-Miranda could hardly have imagined a more perfect day, except perhaps if her father and Uncle Lawrence had been there too. For now she was enjoying the surprise of having her mother and aunt, and of course Lucinda and her friends, together in Paris. She was bubbling with excitement about Aunt Charlotte's baby news too.

Last night she'd thought and thought about that photograph of Monsieur Christian's wife but in the end decided that she must simply look like someone else.

The group wandered along the Boulevard St Michel, poking their heads into the shop windows and looking at the Parisians going about their business, until Cecelia led them through a grand entrance into a spectacular garden. They stopped to take in the view.

'Whoa! What is this place?' Lucas asked.

'Well, it says here that it's the Jardins Du Luxembourg, which I think means the Luxembourg Gardens. There's a palace too,' said Millie. She pointed at the stunning chateau in the middle of the grounds and then went back to scanning her guidebook. 'It used to be for the royal family but now it's part of the government – the building, anyway – and the rest is for the general public.'

'You're very well informed, miss,' Cecelia told the flame-haired child.

'We couldn't go anywhere without her,' added Jacinta. 'She knows more about Paris than the rest of us put together.'

Millie grinned sheepishly. She'd been worried that the other kids were getting sick of her and her guidebook.

'Thanks for bringing us here,' said Charlotte as she linked her arm through her sister's. 'I loved this place when we were younger and I haven't been here in years.'

The group walked further into the park. There was a pretty area with trees and a bandstand, a long water feature with an ornate fountain and loads of open space.

'All right, children, gather round. The park is huge but it should be quite safe for you to explore without the two of us hovering. I think Charlotte and I will pop into the cafe over there and grab some drinks and then we'll find a sunny spot down by the lake. They have little sailing boats for hire. It might be fun to have a regatta later,' Cecelia suggested.

'Just like New York, Mummy, in Central Park,' Alice-Miranda fizzed. 'We could have a race.'

'Cool,' Lucas replied.

Lucinda grinned. She was so thrilled to be in Paris with Alice-Miranda and her friends from school. She could hardly imagine that this was really her life.

'Yes, darling, that's a great idea. Why don't you have a look around and then meet us by the lake in an hour,' said Cecelia. 'Just stay together and don't leave the park.'

The children nodded. Some free time sounded like heaven.

'Who has a watch?' Cecelia asked.

'We all do,' Jacinta said, holding up her left arm. 'We had to have them for the trip so we wouldn't be late anywhere.'

'Good thinking,' Cecelia replied. She glanced at her own wrist. 'All right, then. We'll see you at half past eleven. We have to be back by four so there's time for you to get ready to go to Notre Dame.'

The children raced off into the grounds with Alice-Miranda and Millie leading the way.

'Hey, wait for me,' Sloane grumbled.

They stopped outside the front of the palace. 'Where do you want to go first?' Millie asked.

'What's there to look at?' Lucas replied.

'Well, there are some tennis courts and a basketball court,' Millie said.

'But we haven't got any equipment,' Sloane sniped.

Millie scanned the rest of the page. 'There are loads of statues and things to look at.'

'Boring.' Sloane rolled her eyes.

'We could play hide and seek, if we just stay in one area,' Sep suggested.

'How old are you, big brother?' Sloane shook her head. Something seemed to have put her in a spectacularly unpleasant mood in the past few minutes.

'Are you all right, Sloane?' Alice-Miranda asked. She noticed that Sloane was wearing sandals. 'Is it your blisters?'

Everyone else looked at Sloane's feet too.

'What did you wear those for?' Sep asked. 'You complained all of the first day when you had them on.'

Sloane pulled a face at her brother. 'I thought I might have worn them in and my blisters had started to go away. I wanted to look nice, like all these Paris people. You don't see them wearing daggy sandshoes.'

Lucinda Finkelstein slipped her backpack off her shoulders and fished around inside. 'Here.' She passed Sloane two large bandaids. 'I always get blisters too.'

Sloane smiled at the frizzy-haired girl. 'Thanks.'

'Mrs Winterbottom in training?' Lucas joked.

'Who's that?' Lucinda asked.

'Our headmaster's wife. Her backpack is like a Tardis. She gave Sloane bandaids on our first day too. And the other day Jacinta stepped in a giant dog poo and Mrs Winterbottom came to the rescue with wet wipes, rubber gloves and a disposable face mask, like a cross between a nanny and a handyman. We're still wondering what else she carries around with her.'

'Oh, don't remind me about that,' Jacinta wailed. 'It was gross.'

'You know, yesterday she pulled out a paper-clip for Mr Trout, throat lozenges for Miss Grimm and a giant safety pin for Figgy when the button on his pants popped off,' Millie laughed. 'I'm just waiting for her to whip out a fold-up bicycle or an electric car.'

The children giggled.

Sloane put the bandaids in place and her mood went from fug back to fizz almost immediately. She and Lucinda struck up an easy conversation and Sloane told her all about her ambitions to go to New York. By the time the group reached the avenue of trees at the other end of the park, Lucinda had invited Sloane to stay with them whenever she came to the United States.

'Look, they're playing boules,' said Alice-Miranda. She was pointing at a group of elderly gentle-men who were standing in a flat rectangular area with a low wall around it. Silver balls were strewn around the red granite surface.

'What's that?' Sloane asked.

'I think the particular game they're playing is called pétanque and it's sort of like lawn bowls,' the child explained. 'We play it at home sometimes, but I'm not entirely sure of the rules.'

The children approached the game to watch. Alice-Miranda noticed another set of balls sitting to the side.

'*Bonjour*, monsieur,' she said to a gentleman wearing a red beret, who was waiting for his turn.

He smiled back at her. '*Bonjour.*'

'*Anglais?*' she asked.

The man shook his head. He didn't speak English. Alice-Miranda pointed at the wooden box and then at her friends and in a swift series of actions managed to establish that they could indeed borrow the pétanque set and have their own game on the vacant court beside his group.

Fortunately Millie's guidebook also had a section on traditional French games, and within a few minutes she had outlined the rules and two teams were established. As there were seven children, they needed someone to sit out each time. Millie volunteered to be first as she could help with any questions about the rules.

'So you need to throw the little ball up into the

air and then the rest of you each gets a turn . . .'

Lucas's team won the first round. Lucinda volunteered to sit out the second round. She was watching her new friends when she realized that someone else was doing the same thing. A young fellow with white-blond hair and blue eyes was standing off to the side and seemed engrossed in their activity. At home she would have ignored him completely as she rarely spoke to boys unless they were her brothers. But there was something about being in Paris that gave Lucinda a burst of confidence.

'*Bonjour*,' she said and smiled at the lad.

He nodded.

'Do you live here in Paris?' Lucinda asked.

The boy nodded again.

'It's a beautiful park,' she said.

'*Oui*, mademoiselle,' he whispered.

'Do you come here often?' Lucinda asked.

He shook his head. 'I don't get out very much.'

'Oh, I didn't either until I met Alice-Miranda. She's the girl over there.' Lucinda pointed. 'I used to be like a prisoner until she helped me escape.'

'Escape?' The lad furrowed his brow.

'My papa didn't let me go anywhere but now he's brought the whole family to Paris for a holiday and I have Alice-Miranda to thank for that,' said Lucinda.

'I am like a prisoner too,' he said, and looked into Lucinda's eyes before glancing away shyly again. 'But not today. Today I am as free as a bird.' Fabien's heart skipped a beat as he said this. He hoped that his mother was as busy as he thought she would be.

There was a cheer as Alice-Miranda's team was declared the winner of the second round.

'Lucinda, your turn,' the tiny child called. Then she noticed the young man standing nearby. He looked about fifteen or sixteen. '*Bonjour.* We could do with another player,' she said as she jogged towards Lucinda. She held her hand out to the boy. 'My name is Alice-Miranda Highton-Smith-Kennington-Jones and it's very nice to meet you.'

'*Bonjour*, mademoiselle,' he replied, taking her little hand into his.

'Oh, your hands are so soft,' she exclaimed. 'What's your name?'

'Fabien,' he said.

'Would you like to play with us?'

'*Oui*, mademoiselle,' he responded. 'I would like that very much.'

Alice-Miranda grabbed him by the arm and led

him towards her friends. 'Everyone, this is Fabien and he's going to join us.'

Sep turned around from where he was retrieving the last silver ball. He looked at the lad and wondered why he seemed familiar. And then he remembered.

'You're the boy from the window,' Sep said. 'Across the road.'

Fabien smiled and shrugged.

The younger boy pointed to himself. 'I'm Sep.'

The other children said their names too. Fabien nodded politely and repeated each one.

'That's weird, isn't it,' Sep whispered to Lucas. 'He's that guy. The face in the window. It's strange that we should meet him here.'

'Oh well, you know what they say, the world's a small place,' Lucas replied.

Sep was not quite convinced. He wondered if they'd been followed.

With Fabien's help, Lucas's team won the next two rounds.

The children lined up for another game. Jacinta was gazing dreamily at Lucas, who had proven himself quite the star pétanque player, when she lost her grip on the ball she was holding under her chin. She tried to catch it on the way down but it hit her big toe with a thud.

'Ow!' Jacinta cried. 'Ow, ow, ow.' She jumped around on her good foot.

'What did you do that for?' Lucas rushed to help her limp to the seat near the edge of the court.

'Like I did it on purpose,' she wailed. Her toe was throbbing and tears formed in the corners of her eyes.

Millie raced over and loosened Jacinta's shoe-laces. She slipped off her shoe and sock too.

Sloane leaned in to take a look. 'Yuck! Your big toe is a mess. And your nail is squished and there's blood!'

Sep groaned. 'Way to go, Sloane. Good thing you're not smart enough to be a doctor.'

Sloane poked her tongue out at him.

'But I can't be injured.' Jacinta began to cry. 'I've got the gymnastics championships next month.'

'And you have to sing tonight,' Sloane reminded her. 'Maybe you won't be able to.'

'Sloane, don't say that,' Millie mouthed.

Alice-Miranda knelt down to take a look. 'I think we should find Mummy and Aunt Charlotte. I'm sure it's nothing serious but it's better to be on the safe side.'

Millie and Lucinda volunteered to go and locate the grown-ups.

'Where'd Fabien go?' Sep asked.

The lad who had been playing with them seemed to have disappeared. The children looked around but he was gone.

Jacinta was crying quietly. Her toe was throbbing like a drumbeat and she was making herself sick with worry about the gymnastics competition. As it was, she'd been concerned about taking the week off from training.

The elderly gentlemen who had been playing on the court beside the children wandered over one by one. They leaned in to take a look at Jacinta's toe and shook their heads, except one old fellow who did speak English. 'Those balls are heavy, especially when they hit your foot,' he observed. 'Probably broken. I will call an ambulance.'

'Oh no, sir, that's not necessary. My mother and aunt are here in the park. Millie and Lucinda have gone to find them so we'll be fine,' Alice-Miranda said.

Jacinta began to cry louder. 'I'm not going in an ambulance. I just need some ice.'

'But she needs a doctor,' the man insisted.

'No, monsieur, please, I'm sure Jacinta will be fine,' Alice-Miranda replied.

'Well, she is big crybaby,' he said with a shrug and walked off.

'Rude!' Sloane said indignantly.

Lucas pulled a clean handkerchief from his pocket and sat down beside Jacinta. She leaned her head on his shoulder and he reached out and held her hand. Jacinta sniffed and, despite the pain in her toe getting worse, she allowed herself a small smile.

Millie and Lucinda came running back with Cecelia in tow. Charlotte was taking it more carefully.

'Oh darling, you poor thing.' Cecelia knelt down to examine Jacinta's injured toe. It was noticeably swollen and beginning to turn black, and there was a small cut too. 'I think we should get you to a hospital to be on the safe side. We'll take you in a taxi and then I'll call your mother.'

Jacinta shook her head. 'She can't do anything. She's at home.'

'Perhaps.' Cecelia smiled tightly. Turning up to see her daughter in hospital was the least Ambrosia could do, Cecelia thought to herself.

Charlotte reached the group. 'Oh dear, are you all right, Jacinta?' she asked.

Jacinta began to cry again.

'We can't take everyone to the hospital, Mummy. How about you and I take Jacinta and then Aunt Charlotte can walk everyone back to the hotel,' Alice-Miranda suggested.

Charlotte nodded. 'I'll get us all some lunch and we can still hire the boats if you like. Then we can meet Cee and the girls later,' she said, glancing around at the children.

Lucas looked at Jacinta. 'I'll come with you, if that's OK.'

'I think that's a great idea,' Alice-Miranda agreed. 'Maybe I should stay and take care of Aunt Charlotte. Plus, it's terribly mean of me to leave you too, Lucinda, when I asked you to come today.'

'No, you should go,' Lucinda protested. 'I'm sure that Millie and Sloane and Sep will take good care of me. And Mama and Papa said that we could go to mass at Notre Dame to watch your performance tonight, so I'll see you again before we leave.'

Alice-Miranda rushed over to hug her friend. Then she hugged Millie and Sloane, and Sep too for good measure.

Jacinta managed to get to her feet. With Cecelia on one side and Lucas on the other, she hobbled the short distance to one of the park exits. Alice-Miranda hailed a taxi and soon enough they were speeding towards the hospital, the Hôtel-Dieu de Paris, just by Notre Dame.

Chapter 30

The rest of the school group was out when Charlotte, Millie, Sloane, Sep and Lucinda returned to l'Hôtel Lulu. Monsieur Crabbe explained that the others had gone for a short walk to some nearby markets and would be back soon. Madame Crabbe decided that Charlotte looked tired and immediately set about making her a cup of tea. Lucinda's parents weren't expecting her yet, so Charlotte would take her back to the hotel later. Millie and Sloane invited Lucinda upstairs with them.

The girls were planning to show off their rooms.

'Jacinta's and my room is enormous,' Sloane boasted. 'But you can't swing a cat in Millie and Alice-Miranda's.'

'That's probably a good thing,' Lucinda grinned. 'I don't know if many cats enjoy that really.'

'Ha ha, very funny,' said Sloane. Alice-Miranda was right about Lucinda being a lovely girl, she thought.

Sep decided to head over the road to see if Fabien was there. He was still a little confused about whether the lad actually lived there or if he was just visiting. Sep thought he might want to hang out for a while. Maybe they could play chess in the hotel courtyard until the others got back.

He stood at the door and rang the buzzer. Sep waited a while before pressing it again, wondering if this time there really wasn't anyone home.

He was about to walk away when the door opened and the woman he had met the day before peered around it. Her hair was much messier and there were large bags under her eyes.

She peered out to see if he was with anyone. 'Bonjour.' She seemed to look straight through him.

'Is Fabien here?'

She frowned on hearing her son's name. 'Fabien?'

Sep could see into the narrow hallway behind the woman. There was a staircase running up the side and he thought he saw something moving at the top of the first landing. Sep peered inside, squinting into the poor light.

It was Fabien, and he was pressing his finger to his lips and shaking his head. Sep wondered what the lad was doing but was sharp enough to realize that he shouldn't say anything more.

'I . . . I don't know him,' Sep replied.

The woman turned her head.

Sep peered into the house again but Fabien was gone.

'No Fabien here.' The woman had turned back to face Sep. She slammed the door.

Sep could hear footsteps rushing up the stairs inside. He stood back and looked up at the window where he had seen Fabien before, but this time the curtains did not move.

'Weird,' Sep muttered under his breath. He looked up and down the street. There was nobody else about. He didn't feel like going inside just yet and thought it would be OK to walk to the end of the street and back. As he walked down the steps to the footpath, he bent to pick up a button. It was a pretty thing, with letters entwined in the middle. A, G and an F. Sep slipped it into his jeans pocket. Maybe Alice-Miranda or one of the other girls would like it as a little memento of their trip.

The warm sun on his back made Sep feel a little sleepy. He sat down on the edge of the gutter, wondering how long until the others would be back. He couldn't remember how long he'd been sitting there when Professor Winterbottom turned the corner into the street.

'Sykes, what on earth are you doing out here?' the headmaster called. Sep stood up and dusted himself off.

'Oh, hello sir, I was just waiting for everyone to get back,' he said.

'I hardly think it's appropriate for you to be sitting out here in the gutter, son. I thought you were out with Mrs Highton-Smith.'

'We were. But Jacinta had a bit of an accident and Alice-Miranda and her mother and Lucas have taken her to the hospital.'

'Hospital? What happened?' the professor demanded. He was thinking about how much paper-work he'd have to fill in.

'She dropped a pétanque ball on her big toe and it might be broken,' Lucas explained.

'Oh, thank heavens, nothing serious.'

'Charlotte Highton-Smith is inside having a cup of tea with Madame Crabbe – she's probably having her photo taken too.'

The professor looked confused. 'Right. Well, come along and you can tell Miss Grimm and me all about Headlington-Bear's accident.'

Chapter 31

Cecelia Highton-Smith left Jacinta with Alice-Miranda and Lucas, and stepped outside to make a phone call. They had been sitting in the emergency ward, waiting for the doctor to return with the X-ray of Jacinta's blackened toe.

Cecelia called the Ritz and asked to be put through to Ambrosia Headlington-Bear's room, but they told her that there was no one by that name staying there. Odd, Cecelia thought, seeing that when she and Charlotte had seen Ambrosia in the foyer, she was looking like part of the furniture and hadn't mentioned that she was staying anywhere else.

Cecelia tried Ambrosia's mobile next. It rang and rang and then went dead.

'That's strange,' Cecelia said to herself. 'I can't even leave a message.'

'Did you get hold of Mummy?' Jacinta asked as Cecelia returned to the room.

'Sorry, darling. She must be out of range.'

'Yes, you know the phone reception around Winchesterfield isn't very good,' said Alice-Miranda. She hadn't told anyone other than Millie that she'd seen Ambrosia in Paris. She would talk to her mother about it when they were on their own.

'Typical,' Jacinta groaned. She was still wondering if it was her mother that she had seen in the hotel foyer earlier in the week. 'She's never around when I need her.'

'It's all right, Jacinta. We're here,' said Lucas with an encouraging smile.

'Yes,' she sighed. 'Yes, you are.'

Alice-Miranda grinned.

The doctor finally returned with the X-rays and a rather glum face. 'I am sorry, Mademoiselle Jacinta, but your toe is broken.'

Jacinta bit her lip. 'But I have a gymnastics competition in three weeks.'

The man shook his head. 'I am afraid not. You will need to let it mend and that will take at least a month, perhaps six weeks.'

Jacinta's tears spilled.

Alice-Miranda leaned in and gave her friend a hug. 'If you look on the bright side, at least your toe will get better and maybe if you don't have so much training you can spend more time with your mother.'

'If she's not too busy with her old life,' Jacinta huffed.

'You will need to walk on crutches for a little while and I will tape the toe, but no plaster. It is too small,' the doctor explained. 'And you must wear this for protection.' He held up a sculpted boot that was open at the top. 'It will make things much easier.'

'Can we take her home soon?' Cecelia asked the doctor.

'*Oui*, madame. I have given her something for the pain and tonight she must rest quietly,' he replied.

'But that means I'll miss our performance at Notre Dame too,' Jacinta frowned. 'My one and only solo.' It wasn't turning out to be a good day at all.

'I'm sure Miss Grimm will let one of us keep you company,' Alice-Miranda decided. 'You can't stay at the hotel on your own.'

'Don't worry, darling,' Cecelia smiled at the girl. 'We'll work something out.'

Ambrosia Headlington-Bear was busily sifting through a pile of newspapers. She'd traipsed all over Paris before finding the right library. Whoever decided that the French word for bookshop should be *librairie* had something to answer for – she needed archived newspapers, not romance novels, and she wasn't about to find the former in a bookshop. Finally she had found the right place and she was determined to locate the information she needed. But, of course, as she didn't speak or read French, it was going to be more difficult than she had originally thought.

'Excuse me, madame?' Ambrosia approached a tiny woman who was manning the information desk. 'I was wondering if you could help me?'

To her surprise the woman replied in perfect English.

'Oh thank goodness,' Ambrosia gushed. 'You saved my life.'

'Oh my dear, you're not the first. I've saved countless lives by the very fact that I can speak the same tongue. Now, how may I be of assistance?'

'I'm looking for anything that's been written about a new designer called Dux LaBelle,' Ambrosia explained. 'I'm afraid that I really don't know much about him, other than he's up-and-coming and he doesn't seem to have a past.'

The woman motioned for Ambrosia to take a seat at one of the long research tables. She scurried away and returned a few minutes later with her arms full. 'If he's anyone in this city, you should find something about him in here,' said the librarian as she deposited a pile of magazines on the table beside Ambrosia. 'And I'll have a look to see what we have online – it's easier to search the newspapers through the database. I'm afraid that most of the text is in French, but if you come across something you'd like translated I can assist with that too.'

'Thank you *so* much,' Ambrosia smiled. She flicked through the first magazine. It seemed to be a French equivalent of *Gloss and Goss*, but with more fashion and fewer celebrities. There was nothing about Dux in that one, or the twenty others that she scoured. She'd just have to keep on looking. Seriously, who knew that being an investigative journalist would be such hard work? Ambrosia's phone vibrated in her pocket. At least she'd remembered to put it on silent. There were two missed calls, both from Cecelia Highton-Smith. She would call her back later. It was probably just an invitation to dinner. At the moment she had far more important things on her mind.

Chapter 32

Fabien Bouchard slipped between the sheets and pulled up the covers. He closed his eyes tightly and waited. But not for long. His mother's footsteps echoed on the stairs and then he heard the door open.

She didn't say anything but he could hear her approaching his bed. He shivered as though the warmth had been sucked from the room.

'Fabien, wake up.' She sat down beside him and rested her hand on his head.

Fabien roused slowly and yawned. He stretched his arms above his head, then lay back looking at his mother.

'Mama? What time is it?' he whispered.

'It is the middle of the afternoon. You have slept for hours so perhaps you should be getting up now. I want you to begin practising for the show.'

Fabien's mouth was dry. 'I thought you wouldn't be back until the evening. You have so much sewing.'

'*Oui*, but there have been interruptions,' she replied, stony-faced.

Nerves clawed at his stomach. He wondered when she would ask him about the boy downstairs and how he knew his name. But she just stared at him.

'You are a good boy, Fabien,' she said.

'And you are a wonderful mama.' He reached out to hug her.

She narrowed her eyes and kept her arms by her side.

'Mama?' Fabien blinked innocently.

'Do you want to destroy us? To take away every-thing we have worked for?' she hissed.

'I – I don't understand.' Fabien felt as if there were a piece of croissant stuck in his throat.

'Your uncle has trusted you and this is how you repay him.' She stood and walked to the window. 'You think it is more important to play with stupid boys than build our lives.'

'I was not playing with anyone.' Fabien wondered how much she knew.

She scurried back towards the bed. 'You are lying!' she spat. Her eyes were wild and she looked set to explode.

He'd never seen her like this before.

'I . . . I'm not. I don't know what you're talking about, Mama.'

'Get up!' she shouted.

'Mama, please calm down. Please,' he begged. 'I didn't mean to upset you. Uncle Claude told me about your sickness. It was selfish and stupid to go out. I'm so sorry. I just wanted to feel the sunshine.'

Sybilla Bouchard flinched. 'What did you say?'

'I went out, to the park,' Fabien explained.

'No, not that. What sickness?' Lines knitted her brow.

'The reason you never leave the house,' Fabien replied.

'What are you talking about? I'm not sick,' Sybilla retorted, confused.

Fabien decided he would try another way to calm her down. His uncle had explained that she might become argumentative and irrational if her illness was mentioned.

'Of course you're not sick. But perhaps if you just take some of your medicine,' he suggested.

She looked at him, her eyes wide. 'What medicine?'

'The special medicine that Uncle Claude has,' Fabien said.

A gulf of silence divided them. For several minutes there was nothing.

Sybilla Bouchard didn't know what to think.

'Your uncle is the reason we have anything and don't you forget it. If it weren't for his kindness, taking us in, looking after us after your father . . .'

'After my father *what*?' Fabien's voice shook.

Sybilla stopped cold. 'It does not matter.'

'It does matter, Mama. I want to know about my father,' Fabien begged.

'There is nothing to tell. We are dead to him and he is dead to us.'

'But he is my father. I have a right to know,' Fabien shouted.

'We don't need anyone else, Fabien. It is just us.'

Sybilla reached out to him but he turned away. 'I am so sorry. I love you more than anything in the world. I didn't mean to frighten you.'

She stood and paced the room, stopping at his drawing board. She stared at the pages for several minutes before she spied the corner of the old photograph. She pulled it out and spun around.

'Where did you get this?'

Fabien looked up. 'What?'

'This picture. Where did it come from?'

'Uncle Claude,' he replied. 'He gave it to me yesterday when I was stuck. I thought you had sent him with it.'

'You're lying.' Sybilla's lip began to tremble. 'Claude couldn't have given this to you. It can't be true. It can't.'

'He did!' Fabien yelled.

Sybilla cried out, *'Mon amour,'* before she fled from the room, slamming the door behind her.

Fabien wondered what on earth had just happened.

Chapter 33

Mr Lipp asked the children to gather for an unaccompanied rehearsal before they set off for Notre Dame. He was annoyed to learn of Jacinta's accident, particularly as she had a small but vital solo part.

'I don't suppose the child could have injured herself tomorrow, could she?' he muttered under his breath as the group gathered in the courtyard.

'I'm quite sure that Jacinta hasn't broken her toe just to inconvenience you, Mr Lipp,' Mrs Winterbottom tutted.

Harold Lipp checked himself. 'No, of course not.'

'Besides, you have an ample array of talent – I'm sure one of the other girls would jump at the chance,' Mrs Winterbottom suggested.

She was quite right about that, as Sloane was literally jumping about with her arm in the air asking Mr Lipp who would be taking on Jacinta's part.

'I don't know, Sloane. I haven't really thought about it properly yet,' he said dismissively.

'But I know someone who could do it,' she tried again.

'Yes, we'll get to that in a minute. I suppose Ashima has the right tone, or Ivory,' he mused. 'Places, everyone. We're going to attempt a run-through without any accompaniment. And what is that . . . beautiful sound?' He'd been about to say noise when he realized that it wasn't noise at all, but some of the sweetest singing he'd heard in a long time.

Sloane had wandered away to look at the fountain and begun singing to herself.

'Sloane, is that you?' Mr Lipp was stunned. He'd never heard her sing solo before. 'That's extraordinary. How long have you had that voice?'

Sloane shrugged.

'I've just found my replacement for Jacinta's role tonight. I think we'll have to talk to her about you taking over for good.' He winked at the girl, who grinned broadly.

'Thanks, Mr Lipp, but it might be fairer if we share it next time,' Sloane replied.

Sep Sykes glanced at her. 'Seriously, who are you and what have you done with my sister?' he asked.

'Haha, Sep. You know, I wanted this part for ages but I didn't want it like this. It's not fair to Jacinta either,' Sloane explained.

'Wow, Alice-Miranda really is rubbing off on you.' Her brother punched her gently on the arm.

'Not that much.' Sloane thumped Sep as hard as she could.

'Ow!' he cried. 'Real Sloane's back again.'

She poked out her tongue.

'Places, everyone. Let's get this right,' Mr Lipp urged.

A little while later, a taxi pulled up outside l'Hôtel Lulu. Cecelia paid the driver, then helped Jacinta out. Miss Grimm was waiting to meet them in the foyer.

'Hello Miss Grimm,' Alice-Miranda greeted the headmistress.

Jacinta had swiftly mastered the art of the crutches and with the boot in place she manoeuvred herself next to Alice-Miranda and Lucas.

'Hello Alice-Miranda.' Miss Grimm turned to Jacinta. 'You silly sausage. How on earth did you manage to drop a pétanque ball on your toe?'

'I didn't mean to,' Jacinta said with a shrug. 'I just wasn't paying attention.'

Sloane and Millie arrived with Lucinda in tow. 'You were too busy dreaming about Lucas,' Sloane teased.

Lucas's face turned bright red. 'No, she wasn't,' he protested.

'No, I wasn't,' Jacinta agreed.

The other children kept looking at her.

'Seriously, I wasn't. Not then, anyway,' she said.

The others laughed.

'I'm doing your solo tonight,' Sloane boasted.

'Oh,' Jacinta frowned.

'But don't worry, I told Mr Lipp that next time we perform that song we should do the part together,' Sloane said.

'OK. I think.' Jacinta wondered if Sloane was telling the truth.

'You need to get upstairs and rest, young lady,' Miss Grimm instructed. 'Miss Reedy has kindly volunteered to stay behind and look after you.'

When Miss Grimm and the professor had met with the staff over afternoon tea to discuss the incident and ensuing arrangements, Mr Lipp had volunteered to stay back too. Professor Winterbottom had pointed out rather bluntly that as the musical director, it would be a little odd for Mr Lipp to miss the performance.

'And Lucinda, your mother telephoned a little while ago and said that we should take you with us. Your parents will meet us at the cathedral,' said Miss Grimm.

The children were set to leave for Notre Dame at five pm, with the service commencing at six. They would have dinner afterwards. Monsieur and Madame Crabbe had arranged with Miss Grimm to order in pizzas, which Monsieur Crabbe could attend to. That way Madame Crabbe could see the children's performance too.

Cecelia was planning to head back to the hotel to change before meeting the children at the cathedral but Charlotte was nowhere to be seen.

Monsieur Crabbe appeared from the door marked 'Private'. He took one look at Jacinta and shook his head.

'I heard about this pétanque injury,' he said seriously. 'You know, some may laugh about dropping a little metal ball on your foot but not me. It can be a dangerous sport. Especially when you play it with old men like my father, whose aim is very wonky. Poor Lulu was almost crushed by the silly man one afternoon.'

The children wondered if he was serious.

'Have you seen my sister?' Cecelia asked.

'*Oui*, madame. She is in the sitting room with my wife, supposedly having a rest but I think that Camille has probably worn her out with a hundred and one questions. Please, you should rescue her.' He indicated that Cecelia should go through.

'*Merci*, monsieur. I'll just say goodbye to the children first,' Cecelia replied. 'All right, darlings, I'll go and get Charlotte and we'll see you in a little while. And take care, Jacinta. The doctor gave you some strong painkillers, so you really should go and have a lie down.'

Cecelia hugged each of the children and gave Jacinta an extra squeeze. She was more than a little annoyed that Ambrosia hadn't yet called her back. Surely the woman had seen her attempts to get through.

'Bye Mummy,' Alice-Miranda said. 'See you later.'

'Now, I need all of you to head upstairs and get changed immediately,' Miss Grimm instructed the group. 'We have to leave soon and I don't want any delays.'

The children did as they were told. Jacinta and Alice-Miranda rode the rickety elevator up to the second floor, while the rest bounded upstairs.

Sep and Lucas headed for their room on the fifth level.

'So, I saw that Fabien guy again when we got back here,' Sep told Lucas as they walked along the hallway.

'Why'd he leave the park before?' Lucas asked.

'I don't know. I didn't get to talk to him,' Sep began to explain.

'Why not?'

'Because I knocked on the door over there, like I did last time, and the same woman Alice-Miranda and I saw yesterday answered. When I asked if Fabien was home, I saw him on the landing doing this –' Sep put a finger to his lips – 'So I didn't say anything else and the next thing I knew he was gone. She looked surprised when I mentioned his name and just shook her head. Then she slammed the door.'

'That's weird,' said Lucas. 'We know that he lives there.'

'Yeah,' Sep said. 'I wonder if she just doesn't speak much English.'

'Maybe she's hiding something,' Lucas suggested.

'It was a bit strange,' Sep said.

The boys were changing into their school uniforms when there was a knock on the door. It was George Figworth.

'Hey, have you got any spare undies?' he asked, barging into the room.

Sep looked at him quizzically. 'Yeah, um, but why?'

'The prof was just doing a room inspection and he wanted to know where my dirty laundry was and I said I didn't have any,' the lad explained.

'What do you mean you don't have any?' Lucas walked out of the bathroom, where he'd been brushing his teeth. 'We've been away for five days.'

Figgy shrugged.

'Oh gross, Figgy, have you been wearing the

same underpants since we got here?' Sep screwed up his nose.

'I forgot to pack any,' the boy replied.

'Man, you are disgusting.' Lucas reached into his suitcase and fished around for a spare pair of undies. Sep did the same.

Lucas threw his at Figgy. 'And I don't want them back.'

Sep handed over a pair as well. 'Me neither. They're yours to keep.'

'Thanks. You guys are the best. I can't remember how many times I've turned these ones around but they're getting a bit crusty.' He reached down and pulled on the seam of his underpants.

'Eurgh, get out of here, Figgy.' Sep slammed the door.

The boys began to laugh.

'He's gross,' Sep said.

'Yeah.' Lucas shuddered.

The boys finished getting ready and headed downstairs. As the group gathered in the courtyard, Sep glanced at the window where he had seen Fabien before. He didn't know why he cared so much, but clearly something wasn't right in that house across the road.

Chapter 34

Miss Reedy was quite glad to stay behind at the hotel. While it would have been nice to hear the children singing in the cathedral, looking after Jacinta would give her an opportunity to finish her marking and have some time to herself.

Jacinta was lying in bed with her foot up watching the French version of *Winners Are Grinners*. While Miss Reedy generally didn't approve of much television, she thought this was harmless and potentially educational as Jacinta would have to interpret what was going on.

She made herself a cup of tea and sat down on the settee with the compositions piled in front of her. Her own room was about the size of a postage stamp, so it was nice to be able to spread out a little. Jacinta and Sloane had certainly scored the jackpot with their suite.

Miss Reedy worked solidly for an hour before she decided it was time to stretch her legs and check on Jacinta. The girl had fallen asleep, so she turned off the television and pulled up the covers. She wandered to the window. Here she was in Paris, the most romantic city in the world, and yet she still couldn't bring herself to tell Josiah Plumpton how she felt. She didn't know whether he thought of her as just a friend, or perhaps something more. At this rate she would never know.

Down in the street, Monsieur Crabbe was walking Lulu towards the park. He and his wife were a handsome couple, and he clearly adored the woman, even if he did spend most of the time teasing her mercilessly.

A flash of colour higher up caught her eye. She looked into the windows directly across the street on the first floor. The curtains were open and a man and a woman were fussing over dresses; not the type that you would wear in the street, more the sort of thing that Ambrosia Headlington-Bear would be pictured in on the cover of a glossy magazine. They were lining them up on long portable clothing racks. The woman looked up at her. Miss Reedy averted her eyes and walked back into the sitting room. Her cheeks were flushed and she was embarrassed to have been spotted, although she couldn't say why. She picked up another of the assignments on the pile and began to read.

Alice-Miranda and the entourage walked the short distance to Notre Dame. As the group rounded a curve in one of the small laneways, Millie nudged Alice-Miranda.

'Do you see who that is?' She pointed at a woman wearing an enormous pair of sunglasses and a scarf wrapped around her head.

'Yes, of course. It's Mrs Headlington-Bear,' Alice-Miranda whispered. She had pulled her mother aside when they were leaving the hospital and told her that she'd seen the woman in Paris. To her surprise, her mother already knew.

'We need to talk to her and let her know about Jacinta,' Millie said.

'Yes, I agree,' Alice-Miranda replied.

As fortune would have it, Miss Grimm bumped into a colleague from home and the conga line of children came to another grinding halt. Mr Trout and Mr Lipp were already at Notre Dame and with Miss Reedy looking after Jacinta, the supervision was somewhat diminished. At the end of the line, Mr Plumpton was deep in conversation with Mrs Winterbottom and Professor Winterbottom, and Mr Grump had ducked into a shop to admire some artworks.

'Come on.' Alice-Miranda tugged on Millie's hand. 'We won't be long.'

The girls checked for traffic and then scampered across the cobblestones towards the woman. 'Hello Mrs Headlington-Bear,' Alice-Miranda greeted her.

She looked up from the pile of papers spread in front of her as if she was annoyed at being interrupted.

'Oh, hello Alice-Miranda, hello Millie.' She managed a tight smile and shuffled the pages on the table into a messy pile.

'Jacinta will be so glad you're really here,' Alice-Miranda said. 'She thought she saw you when we were at our rehearsal at the Ritz the other day but the lady at reception said there was no one by your name staying there. But of course you are. Mummy said that she saw you too. Are you coming to the cathedral?'

Ambrosia scanned the line of children across the street. 'No, I hadn't planned to.'

'It's just as well, seeing that Jacinta is actually back at the hotel. She was feeling quite sorry for herself but now that you're here I'm sure you can cheer her up,' Alice-Miranda babbled.

This caught the woman's attention. 'Why is she back at the hotel and why does she need cheering up?'

'She had an accident earlier today and broke her big toe. It's nothing too serious but it will stop her from training for at least a month and she was very upset that she'll miss the championships,' the child explained.

'Oh, that's horrible. Poor Cinta.'

Millie saw a piece of paper on the top of Ambrosia's pile and couldn't help commenting when she read the name. 'Dux LaBelle. We're opening his show tomorrow,' she said. 'At the Ritz.'

'Yes, wonderful new designer. I'm right behind

that young fellow.' Ambrosia grinned. She shifted her papers again, covering what looked like some sort of contract. 'Where are you staying again?'

Millie got out her pocket map and laid it on the table. 'We're staying at l'Hôtel Lulu. Just there.' She pointed to the spot. 'Please go and see Jacinta.'

Ambrosia frowned. 'Yes, of course I'll see her, Millie. You and I both know how highly strung Jacinta can be. I'd hate for her to think I didn't care.'

Millie almost laughed. Jacinta was highly strung and everyone knew where she got that from.

Alice-Miranda looked at the notebook and laptop on the table. 'Are you writing something?'

'It's confidential,' said Ambrosia. 'Well, at least for the moment.'

Alice-Miranda and Millie exchanged bewildered looks.

'Don't look so worried, girls. I'll go and see Jacinta now, I promise.'

Alice-Miranda and Millie said goodbye and walked back to join the group.

'What do you think she's up to?' Millie asked.

'It could be anything but at least she said that she'd see Jacinta,' Alice-Miranda replied.

'Maybe it's got something to do with Dux LaBelle,' Millie said. 'She didn't want us to see whatever it was that had his name on it.'

Alice-Miranda wondered too. Ambrosia Headlington-Bear seemed to have changed quite a bit lately but if she was up to her old tricks again, Jacinta would be devastated.

Chapter 35

Jacinta woke up and wondered what time it was. There was a dull throb in her toe but the painkillers had obviously taken effect. From the sitting room, she could hear deep breathing punctuated by the occasional little grunt. Miss Reedy must have fallen asleep. Not wanting to wake her, Jacinta decided that she would head downstairs and see if Madame Crabbe might be able to make her a grilled cheese sandwich. Her stomach was making all sorts of grumbly noises, and she realized she hadn't had any lunch.

She put on her dressing-gown and grabbed the crutches from beside her bed.

Jacinta poked her head around the bedroom door. Sure enough, Miss Reedy was sound asleep. She must have been marking books the whole time. There was one lying open on her lap next to half a cup of tea.

Jacinta managed to pick up her plastic key and fumble to the door and into the hallway without much noise at all. Soon the lift bell tinged and she was hobbling across the hotel reception.

'Mademoiselle Jacinta, what are you doing out of bed?' Monsieur Crabbe turned from where he was dusting the shelves behind the reception desk. 'Does Mademoiselle Reedy know that you are down here?'

'She's asleep and I didn't want to wake her.'

'She will be worried if she wakes up and you are gone,' Monsieur Crabbe admonished her. 'What can I do for you?'

'I was feeling rather hungry and I wondered if I might be able to get a grilled cheese sandwich?' Jacinta asked.

'Ah, you are in great luck. Grilled cheese is my speciality. But of course, this is France, so I add a little ham and it becomes a *croque monsieur. Délicieux!*

You must sit down there while I go and make it.' Monsieur Crabbe pointed at one of the couches to the side of the room. 'Then I will help you back upstairs so we do not upset your teacher.'

The man disappeared through the door behind the reception desk. Jacinta picked up a magazine on the coffee table in front of her and flicked through the pages. She recognized a whole lot of the Parisian landmarks they had visited but couldn't read any of the text as it was all in French.

She was thinking about the mass at Notre Dame when the front door opened and a woman walked in.

'Mummy?' Jacinta said, frowning.

'Oh, darling, there you are.' Ambrosia flew across the room and hugged Jacinta tightly. 'Tell me, are you all right? I heard that you had an accident and had to go to hospital.' She stood back to survey the open boot on Jacinta's leg.

'I'm fine. But what are you doing here?' Jacinta was very confused. 'Cecelia Highton-Smith couldn't even get you on the phone earlier.'

'I saw Millie and Alice-Miranda when they were on their way to the mass at Notre Dame and they told me what had happened and I came straight here to see you.'

'Yes, Mummy, but what are you doing in Paris?' Jacinta glared at her mother.

'I'm here on business.'

'What business? You don't have a business and if you're here spending money that you haven't got, Daddy will be so cross,' Jacinta admonished.

'It's a surprise, darling. A good one,' her mother replied. 'I didn't want to tell you until I'd really done something interesting, but I have a job.'

'You have a *job*? What sort of a job?' Jacinta was imagining her mother parading nanna knickers on the runway at one of the shows. She hoped it wasn't the one they were singing at tomorrow. Surely not.

'I'm working for Fashion Week,' Ambrosia explained.

Jacinta's stomach lurched. 'You're not modelling, are you?'

'Me?' Ambrosia laughed. 'Are you joking? Oh darling, thank you for even thinking I could but heavens no. That would be too awful for words.'

Jacinta breathed a sigh of relief. 'Then what are you doing?'

'If I tell you, you've got to promise to keep things just between us. You can't tell anyone, not even Alice-

Miranda.' Ambrosia looked her daughter in the eye. 'Come to think of it, especially not Alice-Miranda.'

Jacinta was intrigued. Her mother seemed really excited and she couldn't remember ever having seen her look so passionate – except when her father had given her a new sports car for her birthday, and even that wasn't quite the same.

'I think I'm about to unravel a huge mystery,' Ambrosia began. She leaned in close and spoke quietly. 'It's very complicated but if I can get this right . . .'

Ambrosia explained everything. Jacinta was stunned.

'It's just that I still haven't been able to find anything much about Dux LaBelle. He's a complete mystery. Although I did visit his showroom – it was close to here I think, but I'm afraid all these streets look the same to me.'

'Well, we saw a robbery on the day we arrived,' said Jacinta, trying to one-up her mother in the shock stakes.

'Oh my goodness. I knew it wasn't safe for you young children to travel overseas,' her mother fussed.

Jacinta rolled her eyes. 'Mummy, we are perfectly safe – except around pétanque balls. Don't you want to know about the robbery?'

'Of course, darling,' her mother cooed.

'We were on our way to Notre Dame and three police cars sped into the road and Monsieur Fontaine came running out onto the street and said that he'd been robbed. We didn't know it was him back then but it's been on the news and we performed at his show. Well, sort of,' Jacinta explained.

'I love Christian's gowns. They're always so beautiful,' her mother said. 'And he's such a sweet man.'

'There's a big article about him in here.' Jacinta picked up the magazine she'd been browsing through before her mother arrived.

Ambrosia scanned the text but it was all written in French.

Jacinta pointed at one of the photographs. 'Goodness, Mummy, that poor man is missing a finger.'

'Darling, you're a genius! I'd recognize that hand anywhere. That's the man I was talking about earlier.'

Now all she had to figure out was what Gilbert, the man who showed her the LaBelle Collection, was doing in a photograph with Christian Fontaine.

Chapter 36

'This is the strangest church service I've ever been to,' said Sloane as she glanced around. Notre Dame was bursting at the seams with dignitaries, designers and fashion fans. Some were dressed with understated elegance but others appeared to be competing to look the most ridiculous.

Sep nodded. 'We don't know what the service will be like, but the congregation is pretty interesting.'

'Did you see the size of the bow on that woman's head?' asked Millie, giggling at a lady who was in danger of being swallowed by the polka dot append-age attached to her forehead.

'And what about that guy over there with the lime green plus-fours and suspenders?' Sloane was visibly disturbed by the outfit she had just glimpsed from behind.

'That's Mr Lipp,' Millie whispered.

'Are you joking?' Sloane squinted, wondering if she and Millie were looking at the same person.

Despite the outrageous appearance of some of the congregation, the church service was very traditional. When the children sang their stunning rendition of 'For the Beauty of the Earth', the congregation was rapt.

'Oh my goodness, look at those little cutie pies,' one woman remarked.

'But what is that man out the front wearing?' the designer Christian Fontaine asked far more loudly than he had intended.

The Winchesterfield-Fayle teachers were seated in the pew in front of him. Ophelia Grimm turned around and murmured, 'Yes, what indeed?'

The final chorus was something to behold. First was a beautiful arrangement of 'Ave Maria'. Sloane sang the first verse solo. It was followed by an upbeat version of 'Joyful Joyful'. The choristers executed some rather vigorous dance moves, with Ashima, Susannah, Ivory and Madeline adding their own special routine, which was quickly mimicked by the rest of the group. Alice-Miranda spotted two elderly priests bopping away in a corner and nudged Millie. The priests were in the Monseigneur's direct line of sight too. The man drew in a great gasp of breath. It looked as if the fathers were about to be given extra confessional duties. Then he rocked about in his seat, laughing his head off.

During the rehearsals, Mr Trout's organ skills had been recognized by the priest in charge of music in the cathedral. Now, as the service ended, Mr Trout had been given the honour of playing solo while the congregation left the church.

'Well done, everyone,' cheered Mr Lipp as he met the children outside. The fashion luminaries had exited through the front doors and were now besieged by hundreds of paparazzi all clamouring to get the best shot.

'That was fun, Mr Lipp,' said Figgy. The tall boy was grinning and re-enacting some of his earlier dance moves. 'And your pants are wicked.'

'That would be one word for them,' Deidre Winterbottom whispered to Ophelia Grimm.

Cecelia Highton-Smith and her sister had sat with the Finkelsteins and Madame Crabbe. They had enjoyed the performance immensely and rushed through the crowds to congratulate the children.

'Hello Mama, Papa,' Lucinda greeted her parents. She had sat with Miss Grimm and Mrs Winterbottom close to the choir. 'Did you have a good day?'

'Hello Lucinda.' Her father leaned down to kiss her cheek and her mother gave her a firm hug.

'Yes, your father and I have had a wonderful day,' Gerda replied. She held her hand up and Lucinda noticed a large blue stone sparkling on her mother's middle finger.

'Mama, what's that?' She grabbed her mother's hand and admired the ring.

'It's about time your mother had a special anniversary present. Twenty years is long enough to put up with anyone, let alone me,' said Morrie.

'Morrie Finkelstein, you old charmer.' Cecelia winked at him. Even Morrie's brillo pad hair seemed to blush.

Ophelia Grimm was working at top speed to round up the overexcited choristers. Some were complaining of being hungry and it was getting late. Tomorrow would be a big day with the LaBelle show too. 'I'm sorry to break up this happy party,' she called to the families and friends, 'but I'm afraid these children have to eat and we must get everyone back to the hotel. Of course, if you're happy to eat cheese pizzas, you're welcome to join us.'

Cecelia gave Alice-Miranda a final cuddle and said, 'I think we'll pass. I've got some calls to make.'

'And I have work to do too,' Charlotte added.

'But we'll see you all tomorrow at the Ritz. From what I could see of the flowers being delivered this afternoon, the LaBelle show is going to be spectacular,' said Cecelia.

'And we'll pass too, Miss Grimm,' Morrie Finkelstein said. 'Lucinda's bothers, Toby and Ezekiel, have arranged dinner for the family. I think they've walked every street in the Latin Quarter this afternoon looking for the best restaurant for us.'

Lucinda's face fell. She would much rather spend the rest of the evening with Alice-Miranda and her new friends.

'Lucinda,' Gerda scolded, 'please don't look like that. You will see Alice-Miranda again. Your father managed to get tickets to the LaBelle show tomorrow.'

'Oh! That's fantastic.' Alice-Miranda rushed

forward and hugged her friend. Lucinda's mood was vastly cheered by this news.

Final farewells were said and the children fell into their usual formation. As they followed Miss Grimm and Mr Grump through the backstreets of Saint Germain, Alice-Miranda found herself beside Mr Plumpton. Millie and Sloane were walking ahead and seemed engrossed in their conversation, so Alice-Miranda decided that it was the perfect opportunity to bring up a delicate topic.

'Excuse me, sir,' she said as she trotted beside him.

'Yes, Alice-Miranda, how can I help?'

'I was just thinking that it was so sad for Miss Reedy and Jacinta to miss out on tonight's perform-ance,' she replied.

'Yes, indeed. It was a beautiful service. Absolutely unique,' Mr Plumpton said.

'A bit like Miss Reedy and Jacinta,' Alice-Mi-randa noted.

The teacher looked down at her with a puzzled expression. 'I don't quite follow.'

'Well, the service this evening was unique and we all know there is no one else like Jacinta. She's amazing at gymnastics and she's funny and underneath all those tantrums she used to throw there's a good friend with a heart of gold,' Alice-Miranda explained.

'Oh, I see,' Mr Plumpton nodded.

'And Miss Reedy is the cleverest English teacher in the world and she's so kind and loyal,' Alice-Miranda began.

'And pretty.' The words escaped from Mr Plumpton's mouth before he had time to stop them.

Alice-Miranda grinned. 'Mr Plumpton, did you just say what I think you did?'

'Um, ah, yes I suppose I did,' the teacher admitted, blushing.

'May I say something, sir?' The tiny child looked at him earnestly.

'If you must.' Mr Plumpton wondered what on earth she could possibly add to the conversation. He was feeling terribly embarrassed already.

'Miss Reedy likes you too.' Alice-Miranda winked and scurried off to catch up with Millie and Sloane.

Josiah Plumpton gulped. His nose glowed like Rudolf's and inside he was fit to burst.

'What are you looking so happy about, Plumpy?' asked Mr Lipp as he caught up to him.

'Just being in Paris, Mr Lipp. That's enough to lift anyone's spirits, I should think.'

'Yes, I suppose so. Look, I was rather hoping for some advice. I'm planning to ask Miss Reedy if she'd like to accompany me on an evening out on our last night in Paris. I've already asked Prof Winterbottom for the time off and he's agreed. Anyway, you've worked with her for a long time. Do you know if she likes opera or would she prefer a candlelight dinner instead?'

Mr Plumpton gulped. He could hardly believe his ears. 'I . . . I wouldn't have a clue, Mr Lipp. Miss Reedy's a very private woman and I have no idea of her preferred tastes. I'm afraid you'll just have to work that out for yourself. Now if you'll excuse me, I have to ask Miss Grimm something quite urgently.'

Mr Plumpton rushed off towards the head of the line, leaving Harry Lipp walking beside Lucas and Sep. He shrugged and wondered what was so urgent that Plumpy had to run away like a skittish schoolboy.

'Evening lads,' he interrupted the boys' conversation. 'If you were planning to take a girl out for the night, would you go for the opera, or a candlelight dinner?'

Sep almost choked. 'Really, sir? Why are you asking us? We've never taken girls anywhere.'

Lucas smothered a smile and gave Sep a nudge. 'Who's the lucky lady, Mr Lipp?'

'That you don't need to know.' The teacher stalked ahead of them.

'Seriously, who do you think is about to fall victim to Hairy's charms?' Sep asked.

'Oh, that's easy. It's Miss Reedy for sure. Have you seen the way he looks at her?'

'Poor Miss Reedy. I wonder if someone should warn her,' Sep said.

Lucas shook his head. 'Not me. And you shouldn't say anything either. She might like him, you know. I mean, apart from his outrageous clothes, he's pretty talented and he can be funny too.'

'Yeah, especially when he's wearing that orange leisure suit. He's hilarious,' Sep agreed.

Lucas pushed against Sep's shoulder. 'You know what I mean.'

'Yeah, I'm just kidding. Mr Lipp's a good guy.'

Chapter 37

The children arrived back at their hotel to find Jacinta in a much improved state of mind. She told Alice-Miranda and Millie that her mother had been to visit but, as promised, she kept the details of Ambrosia's mysterious new job to herself.

As they tucked into the pizzas Monsieur Crabbe had ordered for their dinner, the children told Jacinta all about the service and the odd-looking attendees.

'And Sloane was amazing,' Millie said and smiled at Jacinta, who'd been allowed back downstairs for dinner. She didn't tell Miss Grimm she'd already had a very delicious *croque monsieur* earlier.

'Yeah, I was awesome,' Sloane agreed.

'Really?' Jacinta asked sulkily. To add insult to her throbbing injury she couldn't believe she'd lost her only solo part in the performance as well as her chance to compete in the upcoming gymnastics championships too.

'She did sing beautifully,' Alice-Miranda confirmed. 'But I'm sure she would rather that you'd been there.'

'Not really,' Sloane said.

'Sloane!' Millie berated. 'Did you hear what you just said? Seriously, you weren't glad that Jacinta hurt herself, were you?'

'I didn't mean it like that,' said Sloane. She'd realized she was fast painting herself into a corner. 'I just meant that it was fun and I really loved it. And I would never have got the chance. Don't be mad . . .'

'I'm not mad, Sloane,' Jacinta said. 'But you'd better have been awesome.'

'I was OK,' Sloane replied. 'Not as good as you, though – was I, Alice-Miranda?'

'You were great, Sloane. And Jacinta would have been great if she'd been there,' Alice-Miranda agreed.

'Are you two all right?' Millie looked at the girls, who were munching on their pizza slices.

Jacinta and Sloane looked up.

'Huh?'

'Well, usually you'd be fighting by now,' Millie explained.

'I don't fight with people who have broken toes,' Sloane said, deadpan. 'It wouldn't be fair.'

Alice-Miranda giggled. Millie did too. Jacinta and Sloane just stared at each other.

'What? Can't we be grown-up sometimes?' Jacinta nudged Sloane who nudged her right back.

'You can be grown-up all the time, if it means you stop fighting,' Millie agreed.

After the chatter had eased, Miss Grimm and Professor Winterbottom outlined the schedule for the following day.

The LaBelle show would start at 11 am but they would need to leave the hotel by nine to walk to the Place Vendôme and have some morning tea before the performance. Mr Lipp and Mr Trout were hoping for another quick rehearsal too, now that all of the seating and decorations would be in place.

'The adults are going to have a short break for some tea and coffee,' the professor said. 'You can either stay down here and chat or go out to the courtyard. We are fortunate to have the whole place to ourselves and I think you can be trusted to do the right thing for half an hour or so.' The professor glared at Figgy and Rufus as he made the last remark.

Sloane looked around at her friends. 'What do you want to do?'

'Let's go to the courtyard,' Lucas suggested. 'Do you feel like some fresh air, Jacinta?'

The girl nodded and Lucas helped her outside, where Monsieur Crabbe was watering the geraniums and Lulu was lazing on the path.

'*Bonjour*,' the man greeted the children. 'Madame Crabbe tells me your performance was spectacular.'

Sep grinned and said, 'It was fun.'

Jacinta and Lucas sat down on one of the benches closest to the street, while Alice-Miranda and Millie leaned down to give Lulu a scratch. Sep was standing nearby and Sloane was admiring her fingernails and feeling very clever for finding a pale shade of pink nail polish that the headmistress had not yet spotted.

'Monsieur Crabbe, do you know the family that lives across the road in the townhouse with the black door?' Sep asked.

The man rubbed his chin. 'I have seen a man come and go many times. He is small and pointy and wears a beret.'

'Have you ever seen a woman there?'

'A woman? No,' he replied.

'Have you ever seen a boy there?' Sep asked. 'He looks a bit older than us, probably fourteen or fifteen.'

Monsieur Crabbe shook his head. 'No, never. But there are a lot of vans coming in the day and night, especially this week.'

Sep frowned and went to the gates. Alice-Miranda followed him. 'What's the matter?' she asked.

'I went to find Fabien when we got back this afternoon but the woman answered and when I asked for him she just shook her head. But I saw him myself! He was inside, but he made it clear that he didn't want me to tell her anything more.'

'That does sound strange,' said Alice-Miranda. She peered up at the windows, looking for signs of life.

'Yeah, I suppose sometimes families are weird,' Sep said. 'Just look at mine.' He began to fish around in his pocket.

'What are you looking for?' Alice-Miranda asked.

'This.' He handed her the button he'd found on the step outside the house with the black door.

Alice-Miranda studied it. 'I think it's a G and an F together,' she said. 'It's very pretty. There's an amazing Italian designer called Giovanni Fernando. Perhaps it's from one of his designs?' She went to hand it back to Sep.

'No, you can keep it,' he said. 'I don't have much use for designer buttons.'

They went back to gazing across the street.

Alice-Miranda wondered what was going on with Fabien. It was all so very odd.

Chapter 38

Charlotte scrolled through her emails before finding the one she had been looking for.

'Rosie Hunter has done it again,' she called to Cecelia a few minutes later.

'What has she written about this time?' her sister called back from her bedroom, where she was getting dressed.

'One of the smaller shows. It's a great piece. I just wish I could meet her.'

'She must be coming to the LaBelle show today. Surely. It's the hottest ticket in town.'

'I hope so. It was really kind of you to get tickets for Morrie, by the way,' Charlotte said as Cecelia walked into the sitting room.

'Yes, but I've had stern words with him about Dux being our exclusive in New York, at least until the collection is larger,' Cecelia explained.

Charlotte's brow furrowed. 'And you think Morrie Finkelstein will abide by that?'

'Oh, yes. Gerda was there when we talked and she is determined to keep him on the straight and narrow. And besides, Morrie still has several of our former accounts who I encouraged to stay with him – even after they learned what he'd been up to.' Cecelia tightened the clasp on her watch. 'Now, breakfast before we head to the show?'

'Oh yes, I'm starving.' Charlotte rubbed her belly. 'I can't believe how much these little guys want me to eat. You know I said that my pants were just a bit tight. When I went to put them on this morning I couldn't get the zip up. I think I'm going to be a whale by the time they're due.'

'You'll be the most beautiful whale in the world,' Cecelia reassured her. 'Come on, let's go and see how much of the buffet you can get through.'

Adele sat at her desk, glancing up at the clock every few seconds. Monsieur Fontaine would be leaving soon and then she would have her chance. The man had called again and asked her to deliver the sketches in a large envelope to a hotel on the other side of the city. The name he gave was Monsieur Fontaine – he would collect it from there. She couldn't believe the cheek of him, impersonating the very man he was stealing from.

It seemed that there was no other way. He promised that once she delivered the sketches, the vicuña would be returned but of course there was no guarantee. If she went to the police, he said, he would make her disappear, and Christian too. He could have been lying but it was not a chance she was prepared to take.

'Adele?' said Christian. She looked up. 'Are you sure that you wouldn't like to accompany me to the LaBelle show? It might be a welcome distraction.'

'No, monsieur, I have a lot of work to finish and I'd like to leave a little early if I may?' she said. She forced herself to smile naturally.

'Of course. Are you all right?' he asked. 'Since the robbery you haven't seemed yourself at all.'

'I'm fine, monsieur. Just a little out of sorts, I suppose,' she replied.

'Have you heard from the insurance company yet?' he asked.

'No, monsieur.' She looked down at her desk.

'Please get onto them. I will need that money soon,' he said. 'And did you have any luck with the surveillance footage from the buildings across the road?'

Adele's mouth was dry. The day before, she had realized that several of the shops across the road from the atelier had security cameras mounted on their facades. But so far, none of them were pointing the right way and the one that would have showed their building was broken. Adele had thought that if she could find out who the thief was and lay a trap, maybe she could get the fabric back without stealing Christian's designs as well.

'Never mind. The police are investigating. There is still some hope.'

Adele had never felt more hopeless in her life. Not only was she now in cahoots with the thief, she was about to steal from her beloved boss, in the hope that she could get back the fabric that she had forgotten to insure.

Christian took his coat off the peg near the door.

'See you tomorrow,' he called.

'Monsieur!' Adele called out.

'*Oui*, what is it?'

She had been about to tell him everything but the sound of the man's voice entered her head: 'I can make people disappear,' he had said.

'Nothing. I will see you tomorrow,' Adele mumbled.

Her phone rang in her pocket. She pulled it out and stared at the screen. It was a private number. No doubt it would be him, with more demands and more instructions.

'*Bonjour*,' she answered, her voice trembling. 'What did you say? You have found something? Some footage, of a man?' Her heart felt as if it might burst out of her chest. 'I will be there in a minute. *Merci! Merci!*'

Adele couldn't believe it. The detective said that they were almost certain they knew the identity of the thief. Now they just had to find him. She would not have to take Christian's designs after all.

Chapter 39

As the children gathered in the courtyard waiting for Mr Lipp, Alice-Miranda glanced across the street. Outside the house with the black door, someone had erected a tent from the doorway to the road, enclosed on all sides. A black van parked against the kerb formed an extra shield. It was the strangest thing.

'I wonder what's going on over there?' Alice-Miranda nudged Millie, who turned to look.

Livinia Reedy had spotted the van too. She smiled to herself, wondering if the gowns she had seen the evening before were so top secret that they required such bizarre transportation.

Mr Lipp appeared at the doorway. He wore plaid trousers in pink and green, a bright blue blazer and a yellow bow tie. A yellow beret completed the ensemble.

Miss Grimm just shook her head. 'Well, come along everyone. Mr Lipp, why don't you lead the way? There is no chance any of us will get lost with such a beacon lighting our path.'

'Ah, well, I was hoping to walk with Miss Reedy,' the teacher replied.

Miss Grimm noticed her English teacher's mouth turn down ever so slightly. 'I think you should come with me. And besides, I've organized a taxi to take Jacinta to the Ritz and Miss Reedy will be accompanying her.' Miss Reedy mouthed 'thank you' to Miss Grimm.

Mr Lipp looked wounded but fell into place beside Miss Grimm at the head of the line.

Half an hour later the group arrived at the hotel. The Place Vendôme was already swarming with paparazzi eager to get photographs of the mysterious Dux LaBelle.

Miss Grimm charged up the front steps and through the crowd. '*Bonjour,*' she said to the security guard, who resembled a statue of Adonis. 'My name is Ophelia Grimm and I have the Winchester-Fayle Singers with me. They are providing entertainment for the commencement of the LaBelle show.'

The man spoke into an invisible microphone and a woman rushed out of the front doors armed with a clipboard and a serious-looking headset. Miss Grimm thought she looked equipped to be flying a spaceship, not running a fashion show.

'*Bonjour*, madame, please bring the children through.'

Miss Reedy and Jacinta had arrived earlier and were standing outside waiting for the others.

Sloane looked over her shoulders and flicked her hair with a broad smile at the photographers. But Miss Reedy saw exactly what she was up to. 'Oh, no you don't, young lady.' The teacher put her hand up to block the man's camera. 'No pictures of the children.' She guided Sloane away by the arm.

'But my mother would be so furious if I ended up on the pages of *Gloss and Goss*,' Sloane griped.

'Yes, and I would be too.' Miss Reedy shielded Sloane with a discarded newspaper she'd picked up from the back of the taxi on the way over.

The palatial foyer looked even more lavish than

on their previous visit.

'This place is ridiculous,' Sloane said loudly. One of the staff gave her a very sour look. 'I mean ridiculous in a good way.'

The children were taken through the long foyer and into the grand salon. The runway was now finished and near the entrance, where the models would emerge, 'LaBelle' was emblazoned in swirly letters on the sumptuous silk curtains.

Rows of duck-egg blue chairs with gold legs would provide seating for the guests, and thankfully the area reserved for the children was larger than Mr Lipp and Mr Trout had been expecting. Unlike at their first show, Mr Trout had a full-sized Steinway grand piano at his disposal.

'You have thirty minutes to rehearse,' the officious woman with the clipboard and headset informed Miss Grimm. 'Then we have a final sound check, so you will need to take the children to the green room.'

Mr Lipp rushed about positioning the children and soon enough they were running through the repertoire and doing very well.

Towards the end of the rehearsal a woman entered the room. She was wearing a red puffball skirt, red striped stockings like something out of a Dr Seuss book and a white blouse with the most enormous bow at the neck. Her lips were also bright red and her hair was teased up on top of her head.

As the final chord rang out, and the other staff members clapped, the woman let out a shrill whistle.

Mr Lipp turned. 'I'd know that whistle anywhere. Saskia, darling!'

The woman rushed over and the two embraced. When she finally released Mr Lipp, he introduced her to the group.

'Everyone, this is my sister, Saskia Lipp. She's the reason we're here enjoying the delights of Paris.'

Saskia beamed.

Mrs Winterbottom leaned over and whispered to Miss Grimm. 'A love of fashion clearly runs in the family.'

The headmistress nodded and then stepped forward. 'It's lovely to meet you, Miss Lipp. And thank you on behalf of all of us for this most wonderful opportunity. The children have had a ball and it's been a lot of fun for us grown-ups too.'

'It's a pleasure.' Saskia shook Miss Grimm's hand. 'Unfortunately I can't stay. There's a floral disaster over at the Didior show. They had a million blooms hand placed into specially built oasis walls and one of them has taken a tumble. I have to source twenty thousand white daisies before three o'clock.'

'It sounds like you've got a challenge on your hands there,' Miss Grimm replied. 'It's been lovely to meet you and thanks again.'

The children chorused their thanks as well and Saskia dashed away.

Miss Grimm directed the children to the green room, which she had investigated during the earlier part of the rehearsal. They went through a set of ornate doors into a rather stark hallway, which was clearly not meant for paying guests to see. There were doors on both sides and another hallway at the end. A burly security man held open the door at the end and ushered the children through. It was a plain room strewn with chairs and with a single television screen mounted in the corner.

'Someone will come to collect you five minutes before the start,' the security man said.

Chapter 40

A heavily tinted black limousine pulled up at the back door of the hotel. Shielded from prying lenses by high walls and heavy security, Dux LaBelle swept out of the vehicle. He wore a black cape with a stunning magenta lining and the top half of his face was covered by a white mask. Another man exited the other side of the car. He was dressed in a blue suit with a matching beret atop his head.

They were met by a uniformed fellow wearing an enormous headset. He bowed slightly. '*Bonjour,*

Monsieur LaBelle. It is a pleasure to have you here at the Hôtel Ritz.'

Dux nodded slightly but said nothing. The smaller man returned the gesture too.

The pair were ushered downstairs into a long hall and directed to a tiny room. Once inside, the suited man turned to Dux.

'I have to go and speak with someone. It's very important. You must stay here until I return.'

Dux nodded and the man scurried out the door.

'Excuse me, Miss Reedy,' said Alice-Miranda. 'Jacinta needs to go to the toilet. Would you like me to go with her?'

Millie raised her hand. 'I do too.'

'You can both go,' Miss Reedy agreed. 'There are some toilets at the end of the hallway, just around the corner.'

The three girls left the room and walked to the end of the corridor. The bathroom was tiny but fortunately it had three cubicles.

Alice-Miranda was in and out in a jiffy and decided to wait for the other two in the corridor.

After a moment, a door opposite opened and a man wearing a cape and a mask walked out. He almost bumped into her.

'*Bonjour*,' said Alice-Miranda. She studied the man. He was tall and lean and his outfit seemed familiar. Suddenly she realized exactly who she was talking to. 'Are you Dux LaBelle? I've heard about your brilliant masks and capes. It's so lovely to meet you. My name is Alice-Miranda Highton-Smith-Kennington-Jones.' She held out her tiny hand. 'I'm in the Winchester-Fayle Singers. We're very excited to be opening your show.'

The man's hand hovered for a moment before finally he reached down.

'My goodness! You have the softest hands,' she whispered.

Dux flinched and withdrew. He folded his arms under the cape. Alice-Miranda studied him for another few seconds. And then she knew.

'Fabien?' She looked at the mask, searching for the eyes that were hidden behind tiny holes. 'Is that you?'

He placed his hand over her mouth and yanked her back through the door he'd come from. He quickly snipped the lock on the door.

Millie and Jacinta emerged from the toilets and

looked up and down the hallway. Alice-Miranda was nowhere to be seen.

'She must have gone back to the room already,' Millie said. But she was sure Alice-Miranda had said that she'd wait for them outside.

Behind the locked door, Alice-Miranda spoke sternly to Dux LaBelle. 'What's going on? Why did you bring me in here?'

The man gulped.

Alice-Miranda looked at him again, wondering if she'd made a mistake.

'Please take off your mask,' she begged.

Dux turned to the wall and pulled off his mask. Slowly, he turned around.

'I knew it was you!' Alice-Miranda clasped her hands together in delight. 'But, you're so young to be a fashion designer. I mean, you're tall but you can only be fifteen or sixteen!'

'That's right. I am fifteen. Are you surprised?'

'Of course. You're amazing. Your designs are so beautiful. One of my friends, Jacinta Headlington-Bear – you met her yesterday – well, her mother wore one of your gowns to a huge awards ceremony a little while ago and she was on the cover of a magazine,' Alice-Miranda prattled.

Fabien looked away.

Alice-Miranda took a step closer. 'Why do you wear that mask?'

'I don't really know,' Fabien replied. 'It is Uncle Claude and Mama's idea. I have to be a mystery. They say no one must know. I will be more famous because of the intrigue.'

'You live across the road from the hotel where we're staying, don't you?'

'*Oui*,' he said. 'But my mama is unwell and I never really leave the house. When I saw you at the park yesterday it was the first time I had escaped.'

'Escaped?' Alice-Miranda was shocked.

'I'm not allowed out. My mother is terrified that something bad will happen to me so I can only go out with my uncle but he is away on business most of the time.'

Before Alice-Miranda could ask him anything else, they were both distracted by the blare of a news bulletin on the TV mounted to the wall. There was grainy footage of a man wearing a beret and carrying something. Then there was a picture of the designer Christian Fontaine.

'That's Christian Fontaine. We sang at his show. He was robbed of some very expensive fabric a week or so ago,' the child said. 'We saw him outside his studio with the police.'

The footage changed back to the grainy CCTV shot of the man.

Fabien stared. He stood up and walked closer to the television. 'No! It can't be!'

'What? What's the matter?' Alice-Miranda looked at the boy, then back at the screen.

The shot zoomed in.

Fabien gasped. 'That man is my uncle.'

'But how can you tell?' asked Alice-Miranda.

Fabien held up his hand. 'My uncle lost his middle finger in an accident when he was a boy. And I would know that hand anywhere. But how . . .' The boy's face drained of colour. 'He is a thief?' Fabien took a few moments to digest the news.

'Are you sure it's him?' asked Alice-Miranda.

'Uncle Claude told Mama that there would be a van arriving to pick up some stock from the basement. He told her that it was very important – he must be getting rid of the fabric.'

'You don't think your mother knows about this, do you?' said Alice-Miranda.

'No,' Fabien shook his head firmly.

'And where is your uncle now?' Alice-Miranda asked.

'He's upstairs doing some business.'

'We could call your mother,' Alice-Miranda suggested.

There was a telephone on a corner table. Fabien picked up the receiver to dial and then stopped.

'What's the matter?' asked Alice-Miranda.

'I . . . I don't know what the number is,' he said, frowning. 'I've never called it before.'

'Don't worry.' Alice-Miranda patted the young lad on the shoulder. 'We'll find another way to contact her.'

'We have to go there. Now, before Uncle Claude comes back.' Fabien turned and walked towards the door.

'But you can't miss the show!' said Alice-Miranda. She looked Fabien up and down. 'I have an idea.'

Millie and Jacinta returned from the toilet to the green room.

Miss Grimm and Mrs Winterbottom had gone off in search of the morning tea the group was promised before the parade, and Mr Trout and Mr Lipp had disappeared to do the sound check.

The children were sitting in pairs and small groups, some talking, others playing cards and games they'd been smart enough to bring in their daypacks. The girls joined Sep, Lucas and Sloane, who were watching the television in the corner.

'Have you seen Alice-Miranda?' Millie asked.

'No, I thought she was with you,' Sloane replied.

'She was,' said Millie. 'Perhaps she went upstairs to see her mother and aunt. Hey, that's Christian Fontaine, the guy we were supposed to sing for at Versailles.'

The others looked up and saw a flash of the parade in the Hall of Mirrors and then the footage changed to the CCTV images.

'I wonder if that's the guy who stole that expensive llama fabric,' Millie said. There was something about the man on the screen that niggled at Millie but she wasn't sure what.

Miss Grimm and Mrs Winterbottom returned empty-handed from their morning tea expedition and neither of them was happy about it.

'Children, apparently you're needed for a final, final rehearsal. They've had to move some things around at the last minute and Mr Trout's a little anxious,' announced Miss Grimm. Several more rows of chairs had been brought in and it looked like the children's performance space had been depleted.

'Anxious? That's being rather kind, dear,' Deidre Winterbottom whispered to her friend. 'Apoplectic is more like it.'

The children followed Miss Grimm and Mrs Winterbottom along the hallway towards the salon. Jacinta and Millie were last, with Jacinta hobbling on her crutches. Sep and Lucas were just ahead with Sloane.

'Psst,' a voice called.

Millie spun around and saw Alice-Miranda poking her head out of a doorway. Sep heard it too.

'What are you doing?' Millie asked.

'Come here,' Alice-Miranda whispered urgently. Sep tapped Lucas on the shoulder and he and Sloane stopped and turned around too.

'What are you doing, Alice-Miranda?' Sloane called.

Sep clamped his hand over his sister's big mouth. 'Shh, come on.' He directed Sloane, Lucas, Millie and Jacinta to fall behind the rest of the group. Fortunately Mrs Winterbottom had been distracted by an awful smell, which Figgy and Rufus were each claiming as their own.

'You lads are utterly disgusting,' Mrs Winterbottom crowed. 'I'm so glad the professor and I don't have to board with you lot any more.'

Alice-Miranda's friends piled into the room, which was a smaller version of the one they'd just come from.

'What are we doing in here?' said Sloane impatiently. 'You know they'll be looking for us in a minute.'

Sep noticed the lad standing in the corner. 'Fabien? What are you doing here?'

'He's Dux,' Alice-Miranda answered on the boy's behalf. 'Dux LaBelle.'

'What?' the group looked at each other.

Alice-Miranda and Fabien explained their suspicions about Claude as quickly as they could.

'We have to call the police,' said Sloane.

'There's no time. Uncle Claude said that there was a van coming this morning to collect a whole lot of old fabric from the basement storeroom.'

'Is it really that big a deal?' Sloane said. 'I mean, it's just some fabric.'

Jacinta shot her friend an indignant look. 'It's not just *some* fabric, Sloane. It's the world's most expensive cloth and he stole it.'

'You don't know that for sure,' Sloane said. 'It might be a coincidence.'

'I don't think so. There's something I haven't told you. My mother has a new job and she's here writing stories for Fashion Week,' Jacinta began.

'See, I told you your mother might get a job one day,' Sloane gloated.

Jacinta ignored her. 'She went to visit Dux LaBelle's showroom earlier in the week and she met a man called Gilbert, but I think he's the same person that you're calling Claude.'

'How do you know that?' Alice-Miranda asked.

Jacinta glanced up at Fabien. 'Well, you said that your Uncle Claude is missing a finger and Mummy said that this man Gilbert was too. It would be a pretty strange coincidence to have two people connected to Dux who have missing fingers.'

Fabien's jaw dropped. He'd once heard his uncle answer the phone and say that his name was Gilbert. When he'd asked him about it, Claude had said that if it was good enough for Fabien to have an alias then why shouldn't he have one too. He said that it was part of the game of being in fashion – like theatre. It was all a show. Fabien had thought it was a little strange at the time but so were a lot of things about his life.

'It's him for sure,' Fabien confirmed. He told the children what he knew about his uncle's other name.

'But why was your mother writing a story about Dux?' Lucas asked.

'Well, he's such a mystery – I mean, *you're* such a mystery, Fabien. Mummy thought she could get the scoop and then she would really make a name for herself as a writer. But when she started to investigate, Mummy and I found an old photograph in a magazine with your uncle and Monsieur Fontaine. So she was trying to find out about the connection.'

'And did she?' Millie asked.

'I'm not sure. I haven't seen her again.'

Fabien was growing impatient. 'Please, we have to do something.'

Suddenly the door flew open and Mr Plumpton appeared.

'What are you lot doing in here? Mr Lipp's up there having a fit because half the choir is missing. Come along now.'

Alice-Miranda stepped forward and looked at the teacher beseechingly. 'Mr Plumpton, we need your help. You see . . .' And she explained the situation once more.

'Oh my, but what about the show?' exclaimed

Mr Plumpton. 'People will be expecting to see you, Dux – Fabien – whatever your name is.'

'I've got an idea, sir.' Alice-Miranda pulled on his shirtsleeve. The teacher leaned down and she whispered in Mr Plumpton's ear.

'Do you think he could pull it off?' The teacher gave her a dubious look.

'I'm sure he'd love it,' she said. 'He's about the same size.'

'What? Who?' Millie asked.

'I've got a limousine at the back door,' said Fabien. 'Come on.'

Jacinta looked at her swaddled foot and pulled a face. 'I'll just slow you all down. I'll stay and explain everything to Miss Grimm and the professor.'

'All right. You, you, you and you,' said Mr Plumpton, pointing at Jacinta, Sloane, Millie and Lucas, 'head to the rehearsal and don't breathe a word of this to anyone. And I'll be back in a minute. Give me that.' He pointed at the mask in Fabien's hand. 'And the cape too. Hurry up, lad.'

Fabien handed them both over to the Science teacher, who raced out of the room.

'Don't go without me,' Josiah Plumpton called back.

Chapter 41

Sybilla Bouchard didn't want to believe what Fabien had told her about the photograph she'd found on his drawing board. Thankfully he hadn't recognized the young woman in the picture with the flowing red hair. But that had been such a long time ago. And how could she possibly ask Claude without stirring up painful old memories? She waited until Claude and Fabien left for the show, then went to her brother's room. But there was nothing. Then she remembered the basement. Claude was always back and forth down there, although she didn't much care to visit it herself. What secrets could it hold? He'd never told her that she couldn't go down there; he just saved her the bother by bringing up the things she required.

Sybilla realized that she would have to leave the house – in the daylight – if only to walk the few steps to the black door that led into the subterranean rooms. She opened the front door and checked left and right before closing it behind her and scurrying down the stairs to the level below. The door was locked but she knew her brother left a key out for the delivery man who came and went at odd times of the day and night. She felt around for it behind the loose grate and opened the lock. He was predictable – their father had used a similar hiding place for keys when they were children. The room was dark but didn't smell damp as she expected it might.

Sybilla closed the door behind her and felt about for a light switch. A single bulb cast a dull glow over the room. She had never seen so much fabric. There were shelves lining the room stacked high with coloured silks and cashmeres, acetate linings and just about any other cloth you could imagine. It was certainly more than they would need for years to come. She knew that her brother was keen to expand the business but this was outrageous. Sybilla poked about for a few minutes, wondering how they could afford to have so much stock – and such beautiful quality. Her heart beat like a drum inside her chest.

There were several doors leading off the main room. She opened one and found another room with yet more fabric. She tried another room. This one was empty except for an old timber blanket box with a large padlock. Sybilla jangled the latch and looked around for something she could use to break it open. Her eyes came to rest on an old iron doorstop. Sybilla struggled to pick it up and then slammed it down as hard as she could on the padlock. It sprung open and she dropped the doorstop back onto the floor with a loud thud.

Sybilla had no idea what sort of Pandora's box she was about to open. She prised up the lid and stared. Surely her eyes were deceiving her. The box was full of photographs and sketches. Her hand dug deeper until she pulled out a bundle of letters that made her cry out loud. The bundle was tied neatly together with a ribbon, and she recognized her own handwriting on the top envelope.

Sybilla's legs collapsed underneath her. The fistful of letters she was holding spewed from her hands and scattered across the floor.

Her mind was numb. How could her brother have done this to her – and to his nephew too?

Fat tears formed in the corners of her eyes, then ran in rivers down her cheeks. She was sobbing so loudly she didn't hear the door unlatch.

The men hadn't been expecting company. They had a routine: get in, clear out and go, then do it all over again in another few weeks' time. As long as the woman didn't see anything there was no need for anyone to get hurt. It would be a simple burglary.

Sybilla didn't hear the man behind her until a rough hessian bag was thrown over her head. As her hands and feet were bound and the door firmly closed, she began to wonder what her life had become.

Chapter 42

As Alice-Miranda, Sep and Fabien reached the back door of the Ritz, the older lad raced towards the limousine he had arrived in.

A burly security guard intercepted him, shouting in French, 'What do you think you're doing?'

'It's my limo,' Fabien replied.

'Nice try, monsieur, but this limousine is for the designer, Dux LaBelle.' The man shook his head and eyeballed Fabien.

'But I . . .' Fabien began.

'No! Don't.' Alice-Miranda raced up and grabbed the boy's arm. 'We'll find another way. Come on.'

Josiah Plumpton charged out of the back door, puffing like a steam engine. 'Hold up!' he called.

Alice-Miranda raced into the laneway with the boys and Mr Plumpton behind. There wasn't a taxi in sight and as they neared the Rue de Rivoli the traffic was at a standstill.

Alice-Miranda stopped. Sep and Fabien kept up but Mr Plumpton was struggling.

'I've got a better idea,' called Sep. He pointed at a bank of bicycles.

Alice-Miranda nodded. 'Of course.'

'NO!' Mr Plumpton wheezed. The children stopped in their tracks. They weren't used to him being so assertive. 'Let's take one of those.' He pointed at the row of tiny electric cars.

'Good thinking, sir,' Alice-Miranda agreed.

Mr Plumpton inserted his credit card into the self-serve podium and within a few seconds he was in the car. Sep and Alice-Miranda squeezed into the back seat and Fabien wedged himself into the front.

A moment later the little car was speeding through the traffic, weaving between the other cars. At one stage Mr Plumpton took to the footpath, dodging pedestrians who were diving out of the way.

'Look out, sir, it's a one-way street,' shouted Sep. He held his breath as the teacher sped down the cobbled lane.

From a side street a police siren began to wail.

'Oh my goodness!' the Science teacher said. 'Perhaps we should pull over and let the police go past.'

'I don't think so, sir. It's us they're after.' Sep looked around and saw the policeman shaking his fist.

'Oh, oh, but I've never been in trouble in my life!' Mr Plumpton looked as if he was about to pass out.

'It's just up there, around the corner.' Fabien pointed at a laneway that ran off the main road. The trouble was, Mr Plumpton had to negotiate four lanes of traffic from one side to the other. The teacher wove the little car in and out of the passing vehicles. Only once did Sep close his eyes, quite sure they were about to end up in the back of a garbage truck.

Alice-Miranda looked at her teacher in shock and admiration. 'Where did you learn to drive like that?'

'I once took an advanced driver course, just for fun,' Mr Plumpton replied. 'I never realized it would come in so handy.' He skidded the car to a halt outside l'Hôtel Lulu, with the police car, its siren wailing, right behind him. The officer leapt from the vehicle and was stunned when the stout little man and three children emerged from the tiny car.

Fabien was the first to speak. 'Please, I can explain everything.' He launched into rapid French.

After some questions and snorts of disbelief, the police officer shooed Fabien away and turned to Mr Plumpton.

Fabien raced to the front door of the townhouse. He tried the handle but it was locked. He rang the bell and waited for his mother to come but she didn't.

The policeman was busy trying to work out what to do with Mr Plumpton. At least the Science teacher had a reasonable grasp of French and was doing his best to explain what was going on.

Alice-Miranda scurried down the stairs to the basement door. She was surprised to find it ajar. 'Sep, Fabien, come here,' she called. 'The door's open.'

Alice-Miranda pushed her way inside with the two boys close behind her. The first room was empty.

Not a scrap of material anywhere. The doors leading off the room were open, except for one.

'Have a look in there.' She pointed towards one of the open doors. Fabien raced ahead and emerged shaking his head.

'Everything is gone,' he said.

Alice-Miranda put her finger to her lips. 'Shh. Can you hear something?'

'It's coming from in there.' Sep pointed at the closed door.

Alice-Miranda tried the handle. It was locked. Fabien looked around for a key but found none.

'Stand back,' he instructed, before kicking the door with all his might. It sprang open. 'Mama!' Fabien cried and ran towards the woman.

He untied her hands and feet while Alice-Miranda carefully undid the knot that secured the hessian bag over her head.

'Mama, oh Mama.' Fabien hugged her tightly.

'What are you doing here?' She wiped the tears from her eyes. 'You are meant to be at your show!'

'It's a long story, Mama, but we have to get back there to make sure that Uncle Claude is arrested. He's a thief.'

'And a liar,' Sybilla added. She looked at Alice-Miranda and Sep. 'You are the children who came to the door this week?' she said tentatively in English.

'*Oui*, madame. It's a long story. We can tell you on the way back to the Ritz,' said Alice-Miranda. She looked at the envelopes strewn all over the floor. 'Do you need all of this?'

'*Oui*.' It would be used as evidence against her brother, Sybilla thought sadly as Fabien helped her to her feet.

Sep and Alice-Miranda set about picking up the papers and putting them back into the trunk.

'But Mama, you can't go out. You're not well.'

'Fabien, I am perfectly healthy, except for the medicine your uncle has been feeding me.'

The boy gulped. 'But Uncle Claude said that you were sick. He said you have agoraphobia and paranoia and that you needed the medicine to calm your nerves.'

'What?' Sybilla's face contorted. 'That's why you think I didn't leave the house all this time and why I didn't let you out either? You think I'm afraid of open spaces?'

'Of course,' he said. 'It's the only thing that made any sense.'

305

'I'm sorry, Fabien. That is a lie and there is so much you don't know. But there is no time to explain now. We must get to the Ritz.' Sybilla turned and snatched up one of the letters. 'This will be enough.'

The group ran out onto the street. With Mr Plumpton's help, Alice-Miranda convinced the policeman to take Fabien and his mother to the Ritz. Mr Plumpton would drive Alice-Miranda and Sep behind them.

In the police car, Sybilla explained to her son that she had been wrongfully accused of theft and fraud many years before. The reason she didn't leave the house was that there was still a warrant for her arrest. Fabian understood now why they had entered France on a private boat and avoided security and customs. Sybilla hadn't wanted to come back to Paris in the first place but Claude had convinced her that he had a plan to clear her name.

Now she doubted that was true at all. His plan was to make money and use Fabien's talent as a designer and her skills as a dressmaker. All her life she had protected him, except that terrible day when he was just a little boy. She hadn't realized that his finger was in the bicycle chain when she had pushed off. She could still remember the screaming. And then their parents were killed in an accident and she vowed that it was her responsibility to always look after her little brother.

Fabien was confused. His uncle didn't need to steal. He had a thriving rug business.

'I'm afraid I don't believe that your uncle has ever sold a rug in his life,' Sybilla said. 'He steals designs and fabric and sells them on the black market.'

'But why did he want me to be a designer?' Fabien asked his mother.

'Money and power, I suspect, and of course you are a huge talent,' said Sybilla. 'How could I have been so blind?' Tears slid down her cheeks. 'All this time I have been hunted for something I knew I didn't do. And it was him, my own brother.'

Fabien reached across and slipped his hand into his mother's.

'Madame,' the policeman in the driver's seat finally spoke. 'I have called for back-up. We will arrest Monsieur Bouchard soon,' he assured her.

Chapter 43

Meanwhile, back at the Ritz, the show was about to start. The room was brimming with characters, mostly female and mostly hidden behind oversized sunglasses and red lipstick. The combined height of their heels would have built a ladder to the moon. Cecelia Highton-Smith and her sister craned their necks to see the children, who were partially hidden behind a pylon and several oversized potted palms.

Jacinta had hobbled up the corridor, intent on finding her mother and making sure that Claude did not speak with Dux before the show. But she had been intercepted by Mr Lipp and sent straight to her position in the choir. When she tried to object and tell him she had to see her mother, he immediately cut her off and said that he was not going to put up with any more nonsense – from anyone. Clearly the last-minute changes to their performance space had done nothing for his mood.

The lights dimmed and Mr Trout began his extravagant introduction. Mr Lipp stood in front of the children and waved his arms about. The children launched into their medley of show tunes, complete with actions.

'Can you see Alice-Miranda?' Cecelia asked her sister.

Charlotte shook her head and frowned.

Cecelia wondered where she was. Millie and Jacinta were there.

Morrie, Gerda and Lucinda Finkelstein were sitting a few rows further back.

'I wish we could see Alice-Miranda,' Lucinda whispered to her mother.

'Never mind, Lucinda. I'm just excited to be here,' Gerda told her daughter. She turned to her husband. 'Why haven't we ever done this before, Morrie?'

Morrie Finkelstein shrugged. Probably because they'd never been to Paris before.

The children's performance was pitch perfect. Mr Lipp looked as if he was about to burst a blood vessel with his intense conducting. A flourish of notes signified the end of the show and the audience responded enthusiastically. Contrary to the running sheet, there was no time at all for the group to exit the room before a soundtrack boomed from the speakers and the first model strutted onto the runway. She wore a stunning beaded gown in fuchsia pink. Her face was hidden behind an intricate mask with plumes of feathers rising from the centre, which made her look at least seven feet tall.

'We're supposed to get the children back to the green room,' Mr Trout fussed.

Mr Lipp just shook his head and signalled to the group to sit down where they were.

The show continued with a procession of beautiful dresses, each one more gorgeous than the last.

Charlotte leaned closer to her sister. 'Dux LaBelle is quite something. I think I'd wear every single one of those gowns so far – and you know usually there are only two or three things that you could ever see yourself in at these shows.'

Cecelia agreed.

The models continued to glide past the audience until finally the statement creation was unveiled, signifying the end of the show.

Cecelia joined in the applause and caught her sister's eye. 'So, what do you think Dux will be wearing today?'

'Surely they can't keep up the mask fiasco for ever?' said Charlotte.

'Oh, I think they can – if the models are anything to go by.' She gestured towards the stream of waifish women charging back onto the catwalk.

And then Dux appeared. He walked down the runway hand in hand with the model wearing the final gown, his head nodding in time with the music. He waved at the audience and even executed a few dance moves.

'Gosh. Don't you remember last year, he barely took a bow,' Charlotte whispered to her sister.

'Another year in the business seems to have done wonders for his confidence, that's for sure,' Cecelia agreed.

Dux turned to walk back along the runway, when out of nowhere a woman leapt onto the stage. She held her hands up like a policeman directing traffic.

Unfortunately, several of the models weren't paying a great deal of attention and there was a rather nasty collision further down the line, causing them to fall like dominoes.

'Turn that music off, now!' the intruder screamed.

'Oh my goodness, that's Ambrosia Headlington-Bear,' Cecelia gasped. 'What on earth is she doing?'

Jacinta also realized that the woman on the catwalk was her mother. 'Mummy!' she shouted.

The DJ sitting off to the side of the runway removed his headphones and looked at the woman.

'Don't just stand there, turn it off,' she demanded.

Flashes went off like a fireworks display from the paparazzi covering the event.

Dux LaBelle stopped his preening and stood awkwardly in the middle of the runway.

A small, rat-like man poked his head around from the curtain.

'Madame Headlington-Bear, what are you doing?' he whispered loudly. He had looked everywhere for her earlier. She had promised to invest in the label and he desperately wanted her cheque.

There were murmurs throughout the audience, with many people wondering if Ambrosia was having some sort of breakdown. After all, there had been rumours that she and her husband had split and perhaps everything had taken its toll.

'Mummy,' Jacinta called. 'I need to tell you something important.'

Ambrosia shook her head. 'It's all right, darling. I think I've got this covered.'

Jacinta wanted to tell her mother about Dux before she made an outrageous claim and ruined her new career as a writer before it had even started.

'I am afraid that we are victims here today. All of us. Victims of fraud,' Ambrosia's voice boomed. There was an audible gasp from the crowd. 'Dux LaBelle is not an outrageously talented designer. He's a charlatan, a fake, and that man there –' she pointed at Claude – 'has done this sort of thing before. Or at least, his sister has. Stealing designs!'

Claude's nose twitched. His eyes darted left and right, looking for the nearest exit. 'Dux,' he called, taking some tentative steps towards the boy. 'Come here.'

But Dux seemed to be rooted to the spot.

'Christian Fontaine?' shouted Ambrosia. 'Are you here?'

The audience gasped again as Christian stood up in the second row.

313

'Hey!' a paparazzo called. 'I saw you on the news an hour ago.' He was pointing at Claude. 'You stole the fabric from him.' Now he pointed at Christian Fontaine.

Claude gulped. He looked at his watch. The fabric would have been picked up by now – his men were very reliable. They would never be able to prove anything.

Lucinda Finkelstein stood up. 'And I think your assistant might know something about the robbery too, Monsieur Fontaine,' she said.

'Adele?' Christian asked, confused. 'She was the one who found the CCTV footage.'

'She is the guilty one,' Claude sneered, then realized he should have kept his mouth shut.

The audience gasped.

Lucinda shook her head. 'I don't think so. When we were at Versailles, Millie and I saw her. She was on the phone and she sounded terrified, as if someone was making her do something she didn't want to do.'

Ambrosia Headlington-Bear was stunned. She hadn't realized her investigation would lead to solving another crime. As far as she was concerned she'd exposed Dux as a fake and nothing more.

'But that's not all,' Jacinta added. 'Alice-Miranda and Mr Plumpton and Sep have all gone with Fabien, who's the real Dux, to intercept the pick-up of that stolen vicuña. I tried to tell you, Mummy, but Mr Lipp wouldn't let me speak to you.'

Harry Lipp gulped.

'But who's that there?' Ophelia Grimm's heart was racing as she pointed at the masked man on the catwalk. She wished someone had told her about all this before now. Heavens knows what was going on with her children out there in the city.

Ambrosia Headlington-Bear strutted towards the lad and pulled off the mask.

Professor Winterbottom almost choked. 'Figgy? What on earth?'

The boy shrugged. 'Mr Plumpton said I'd be doing everyone a huge favour and it seemed like fun, sir. Pretty cool, huh?'

'I'll give you cool, young man!' Professor Winterbottom huffed. But he didn't move; he didn't know what to think.

Everyone was too busy watching the unveiling of Dux LaBelle to notice Claude skulking back down the runway. He dashed behind the curtains and disappeared.

Ambrosia turned around to face the little weasel and jumped. 'Where's Gilbert or Claude or whatever his name is?'

But someone had been watching. There was a loud crash and the sound of a scuffle.

'No you don't, monsieur!' Alice-Miranda shouted.

Every head in the place turned to see what was going on now.

'We've got him!' Mr Plumpton cried. Alice-Miranda and Sep were dangling from the waist and shoulders of Claude Bouchard, while Mr Plumpton had a hand clamped around the man's wrist.

'Let me go, you little monsters,' Claude yelled.

The children jumped off and joined their teacher in marching the dishevelled man back down the catwalk.

At the other end of the salon, the doors burst open. Fabien, his mother and a policeman ran into the room.

'Arrest that man!' Sybilla Bouchard shouted in French as she pointed at her brother.

The policeman made a dive onto the catwalk, where Claude was quickly cuffed. He stood sulking at the audience.

'I just want to know why, Claude.' Sybilla walked up the stairs to face him. 'Why did you do it?' She waved one of the letters she'd found in the basement in front of his face.

'He didn't deserve you,' Claude spat. 'He used you.'

'So you stole from him and made it look like it was me,' she said. Her eyes drilled right through him.

'I had to. You don't know what it's like to be me, Sybilla. You were so beautiful and clever and when you married him, I knew eventually you would dump me. You were so perfect together and everybody loved you. I was nobody.'

'So you built an empire based on theft and fraud and in doing so made sure that my son never knew his own father?' Sybilla demanded.

The French-speakers in the audience gasped.

Sybilla sneered at her brother. 'And this time? Did you steal from him again?'

'Huh! It was so easy. And that assistant of his was so stupid and loyal to him, like a puppy,' Claude scoffed.

'You are despicable, Claude. Take him away.' She motioned to the policeman.

'I'm confused,' Rufus called out. 'What are they saying?'

Mr Plumpton quickly translated the events of the past few minutes for the English speakers among the group.

There was another gasp as they realized just what a wicked little man Claude was.

'My father?' Fabien walked towards his mother.

'Your father accused me of something I didn't do. But I had no proof and I was hurt that he could even think of blaming me. I thought that if I left for a while, he would calm down and we could sort things out. But then I found out that I was pregnant with you. I wrote to your father every week, begging him to understand. To take me back so together we could find out the truth. But I got no answer. I thought he didn't care. That he didn't want to have anything to do with us. But now I know that the letters never even reached him. I found them all today, hidden in Claude's secret trunk with the photographs and sketches he had stolen and the names of all his evil associates.'

'But who is my father?' Fabien asked.

A cough made the audience turn to the tall man with salt and pepper hair, who was walking towards the catwalk.

Sybilla spun around and saw him. The colour drained from her cheeks.

'I think I am.' The man walked slowly up the steps. He held out his hand to Fabien. 'I am Christian Fontaine.'

Fabien reached out to shake Christian's hand and was immediately drawn into his arms.

The whole salon was awash with tears.

'And you . . . my wife.' Christian let go of Fabien and stood back to look at Sybilla. 'For years I have tried to banish you from my thoughts but I have wondered where you were every day.'

Sybilla rushed into his embrace. The audience rose to their feet, clapping and cheering.

Mr Plumpton found himself standing beside Miss Reedy. She brushed a tear from her cheek. 'How wonderful to see a family reunited,' she said. 'It sounds as if they can thank you for helping.'

'I didn't do much at all – just drove the car, really,' he said, blushing. 'But it *is* wonderful to see people in love.' The Science teacher slipped his hand into hers and gave a squeeze.

'Oh, Josiah,' she said, with a teary smile.

'May I take you to dinner, Miss Reedy?'

'Of course. I thought you would never ask.'

The clapping and cheering finally died down and Christian let go of Sybilla. He stepped back and looked around him.

'I am confused about one thing. This collection. Who is the real designer, or is it all stolen?' he asked.

'I am,' Fabien confirmed. 'It's all mine. Uncle Claude gave me a photograph to use for the final gown, but I came up with my own. The photo was of a beautiful creation, but I could not copy it. I suspect it might have been one of yours.'

Ambrosia Headlington-Bear goggled at the boy. 'You're a genius.'

'Yes, my son is a genius,' said Christian. He patted Fabien on the back.

Alice-Miranda scampered over to Ambrosia. She tugged on the woman's sleeve and then whispered in her ear.

'Yes, that's a great idea.' Ambrosia walked along the catwalk and disappeared behind the curtains, returning a few seconds later. She turned to the audience. 'I give you Fabien, the real Dux LaBelle, and his magnificent collection,' she announced.

Ambrosia nodded at the DJ. The music kicked in and the models strutted the runway once more. A cheer went up from the audience and Alice-Miranda

320

and her friends clapped wildly. Fabien smiled. He wondered what life had in store for him next.

But whatever the future held, somehow he just knew that things would work out for the best.

And just in case you're wondering . . .

Claude Bouchard was charged with theft, fraud, extortion and myriad other crimes, including tax evasion. He was destined to spend a long time in prison. Although Alice-Miranda and her friends had been too late to stop Claude's goons collecting the shipment of luxury fabric from the basement, there were witnesses. Monsieur Crabbe had been in the courtyard when suddenly Lulu became very upset, barking and growling. She didn't like the look of the gruff men and their van and neither did he. Monsieur

Crabbe memorized the licence plate number and reported it to the police. The van was tracked to a huge warehouse in Calais right by the port, where Claude distributed his ill-gotten gains. The vicuña was found among a vast quantity of expensive fabric.

Charlotte Highton-Smith was amazed to receive the most extraordinary inside account of what happened at the LaBelle show. Rosie Hunter's writing was outstanding and she seemed to know things that nobody else covering the story did. She immediately put her on contract to write about all the shows for Highton's. She is still hoping to meet her some day soon.

Jacinta was thrilled that her mother had found a new passion. But they agreed to keep it just between themselves for now. Sooner or later it was bound to get out but it was fun having a special secret. The first time Jacinta saw the name Rosie Hunter in a magazine she couldn't have felt more proud.

Lucinda couldn't believe what an exciting time they had in Paris. Alice-Miranda invited her to come and stay at Highton Hall as soon as she could. There was even some talk of a school exchange. Lucinda has her fingers crossed extra tight.

Mr Plumpton and Miss Reedy spent their first

date at the famous Parisian restaurant La Tour d'Argent. It's early days yet, but if Alice-Miranda has anything to say about it, there will be another wedding at Winchesterfield-Downsfordvale before the year is out.

Harry Lipp was particularly put out that his plans to woo Livinia Reedy had failed. However, all was not lost. The lady at the Ritz with the giant headset seemed particularly taken with him, so he asked her to dinner instead.

Adele confessed all to her boss. She felt like such a fool to have been conned by Claude. Monsieur Fontaine was so overjoyed to have his wife back and now a son too that he decided to give her a second chance. After all, didn't everyone deserve one?

Monsieur and Madame Crabbe and Lulu had never enjoyed such an exciting time with their guests. And when Charlotte Highton-Smith said that she would invite them to the premiere of Lawrence's next movie, Madame Crabbe almost fainted on the spot. She immediately set off to the shops to find the perfect outfit – even though the event was a year away.

On their way home from the show, Alice-Miranda remembered the button in her pocket. She pulled it out and examined it. Of course, the first letter wasn't a G, it was a C for Christian Fontaine.

Sybilla and Christian renewed their vows in Notre Dame Cathedral with their son Fabien as the best man. For now, Fabien is back at school. He says he's got a while to decide if he makes fashion his career. But in the meantime, he's teamed up with his father and mother to produce at least one collection a year. Their business, Fontaine and LaBelle, is flourishing.

Cast of characters

The Highton-Smith-Kennington-Jones family

Cecelia Highton-Smith	Alice-Miranda's doting mother
Aunt Charlotte Highton-Smith	Cecelia's younger sister and Alice-Miranda's aunt

Winchesterfield-Downsfordvale Academy for Proper Young Ladies staff

Miss Ophelia Grimm	Headmistress
Mr Aldous Grump	Headmistress's husband
Miss Livinia Reedy	English teacher
Mr Josiah Plumpton	Science teacher
Mr Cornelius Trout	Music teacher

Winchesterfield-Downsfordvale students

Alice-Miranda Highton-Smith-Kennington-Jones	
Millicent Jane McLoughlin-McTavish-McNoughton-McGill	Alice-Miranda's best friend and room mate
Jacinta Headlington-Bear	Talented gymnast, school's former second best tantrum thrower and a friend
Sloane Sykes	Former teller of tall tales and a friend

Ashima Divall,	Friends and choir members
Madeline Bloom,	
Susannah Dare,	
Ivory Hicks	

Fayle School for Boys staff

Professor Wallace Winterbottom	Headmaster
Mrs Deidre Winterbottom	Headmaster's wife
Mr Harold Lipp	English and Drama teacher

Fayle Students

Lucas Nixon	Lawrence Ridley's son
Septimus Sykes	Sloane Sykes's brother
George 'Figgy' Figworth	Rugby player and choir member
Rufus Pemberley	Choir member

Friends of the Highton-Smith-Kennington-Jones family

Ambrosia Headlington-Bear	Jacinta's mother
Lucinda Finkelstein	Friend of Alice-Miranda's from New York City
Morrie Finkelstein	Lucinda's ambitious father
Gerda Finkelstein	Lucinda's mother
Ezekiel and Tobias Finkelstein	Lucinda's elder brothers

Parisians

Madame Camille Crabbe	Co-owner of l'Hôtel Lulu
Monsieur Henri Crabbe	Co-owner of l'Hôtel Lulu and Madame Crabbe's husband
Lulu	Henri's precious dog
Saskia Lipp	PR expert for Fashion Week
Christian Fontaine	Famous designer
Adele	Christian's assistant
Fabien Bouchard	
Sybilla Bouchard	
Uncle Claude	
Dux LaBelle	

Turn the page for lots
more about Alice-Miranda
and friends . . .

How much do you remember about Alice-Miranda's adventures in Paris?

Test your knowledge with this fun quiz!

1. Jacinta calls Paris the 'City of Love' – but what it is its real nickname?

2. What is the name of the singing group that Alice-Miranda belongs to?

3. What hotel are the group staying in while visiting Paris?

4. Which famous star does Madame Crabbe have a crush on?

5. Fabien Bouchard now lives in Paris, but which little island did he come from?

6. And what is the name of Fabien's fashion designer alter-ego?

7. Agoraphobia is the fear of what?

8. What sort of dog is Louis?

9. Name the very expensive fabric that is stolen just before Fashion Week.

10. At the end of the story, which teachers went on a first date at the famous restaurant La Tour d'Argent?

Answers:

1. The City of Light
2. The Winchester-Fayle Singers
3. L'Hôtel Lulu
4. Lawrence Ridley
5. Guernsey
6. Dux LaBelle
7. Going outside.
8. A bulldog.
9. Vicuña, or vigogne in French.
10. Mr Plumpton and Miss Reedy.

Millie's Melt-in-the-Mouth Macarons

Try this delicious recipe for a French treat!

For the macaron shell:

- 150g ground almonds
- 250g icing sugar
- 2 tsp vanilla extract
- 2 egg whites
- Food colouring – choose your favourite, but red, pink, purple and green all look lovely!

For the butter cream filling:

- 140g butter, at room temperature (so soft)
- 280g icing sugar
- 1-2 tbsp milk
- 2 tsp vanilla extract

What to do:

- Preheat the oven to 150°C.

- Line several baking trays with baking parchment.

- To make the macaron shells, put the ground almonds, icing sugar and vanilla into a bowl. Whisk the egg whites until firm and fold in.

- Add 5-6 drops food colouring.

- Spoon the macaron mixture into a piping bag. Pipe little mounds, about 2cm in diameter, onto the trays, spaced well apart. Leave to stand for a couple of minutes until the tops dry, then bake in the oven for 20-25 mins.

- Take out and leave to cool on a wire rack.

- Put the softened butter in a bowl. Add half the icing sugar and beat until smooth. Then add the remaining icing sugar with 1tbsp milk and the vanilla extract. Beat until creamy. Add extra icing sugar to thicken or a little extra milk to make runnier, if needed.

- Sandwich the macarons together with butter cream.

- Enjoy with a glass of milk and share with your friends!

Alice-Miranda's Paris Travel Guide!

There's so much to see and do in Paris! If you're ever lucky enough to visit, here are a few tips:

The Eiffel Tower

The Eiffel Tower is probably the most famous building in France. It's easy to see why! It's the tallest building in Paris, and it's over 100 years old. More than 250 million people have visited it!

The tower is made from iron, and has a very distinctive shape. When it was first built, lots of people loved it – but lots hated it too. One famous French writer even announced that he ate his lunch in the restaurant inside the tower every day, because it was the only place he could enjoy the view of Paris without the tower spoiling it!

Throughout its history, the tower has been home to lots of things: a post office; a newspaper; a patisserie. Nowadays, you can even go ice-skating on the first floor each winter!

The Love Lock Bridge

This is the nickname given to one of the most romantic spots in Paris, the Pont de l'Archevêché (which means 'The Archbishop's Bridge). The tradition is for couples to visit the bridge and fasten a padlock onto it, with their names written on the lock. They then throw the key away, and the padlocks are there for ever!

Even if you don't want to fasten your own padlock onto the bridge, it's still a fun place to visit and take pictures.

The Louvre

This is the most visited museum in the world. It's also housed in one of the most beautiful buildings in Paris: part of it used to be a palace, belonging to a French king. It is probably most famous for the incredible works of art, including the Mona Lisa.

Notre Dame

In English 'Notre Dame' means 'Our Lady'. This is one of the biggest and most beautiful cathedrals in the world, and one of the most famous. It's almost a thousand years old. Many Kings and Queens of France were crowned or married there.

Notre Dame has ten enormous bells that are rung throughout the day. They are all named after famous people in the cathedral's history, or saints. The two most famous – called 'bourdons', or 'Great Bells' – are named Emmanuel and Marie.

One of the most famous French novels of all time is based on the building: The Hunchback of Notre Dame, by Victor Hugo, which is the story of a shy, lonely man living in secret in the cathedral

The Moulin Rouge

In English, 'Moulin Rouge' translates as 'Red Windmill'. But the Moulin Rouge is actually a world-famous dance-hall and theatre. It is very old, and many famous dancers and performers have appeared on its stage. It's where the can-can dance was first invented! Lots of films have been made about it, if you want to find out more.

Did you know . . .

- France has the tallest mountain in Europe, Mont Blanc.

- More than 350 types of cheese are made in France! These include Brie, Camembert, and Roquefort.

- One of the most famous American symbols – the Statue of Liberty – actually came from France! It was presented to America by the French as a president, to show their friendship. One of the people who helped to design and build the statue was Gustav Eiffel – the designer of the Eiffel Tower!

- Some of the most famous books in the world come from France, including Les Miserables, The Three Musketeers, and The Little Prince. Beauty and the Beast was first written by a French author, with a very long and pretty name, a little like Alice's Miranda's: Gabrielle-Suzanne Barbot de Villeneuve.

- More people visit France each year than any other country in the world!

Sloane's Sweet and Sticky Brioche

This is a tasty cross between bread and pastry, and lots of French people enjoy it for breakfast.

For the brioche:
- 250g plain flour
- 100g butter
- 2 heaped tbsp caster sugar
- A 7g sachet of fast-action yeast
- 3 eggs
- A pinch of salt
- 1 beaten egg, to glaze
- 3 white or brown sugar cubes, lightly crushed

What to do:

- Rub the butter into the flour with the tips of your fingers, until your mixture looks like breadcrumbs.

- Stir in the caster sugar, salt and yeast, then add the eggs and mix to a soft dough.

- Cover with a clean tea towel and place in a cold place for twenty minutes (this makes the mixture easier to handle).

- While this is chilling, put a light coating of butter into a 2 pint loaf tin.

- Sprinkle a layer of flour onto a work surface and tip the dough onto it. With floured hands, knead very briefly to form a ball, then drop the dough into the tin, smooth side up.

- Cover with cling film and leave to rise in a warm place for about two hours, until doubled in size.

- Heat oven to 200°C.

- Brush the top of the brioche with egg yolk, then sprinkle over the crushed sugar and bake for 20-25 mins, until the loaf is golden brown.

- Tip out onto a wire rack and leave to cool.

- Slice very carefully, and try with butter and your favourite jam.

Test your French!

Can you match the English word or phrase with the French one? We've started you off!

Hello	Amie
Goodbye	Merci
Thank you	Robe
Teacher	Chien
Friend	Aventure
Thief	Au revoir
Adventure	Professeur
Dress	Bonjour
Dog	Voleur

Get ready for
Alice-Miranda's next adventure . . .

ALICE-MIRANDA SHINES BRIGHT

Alice-Miranda and Millie have made a dazzling discovery in the woodlands near their school! They vow to keep the secret to themselves, but it seems that a greedy politician and a pair of old friends are searching for the same treasure. And back at school, Jacinta is being particularly grumpy with everyone, but no one quite knows why.

So Alice-Miranda puts her detective hat on. It's time to get to the bottom of these mysteries . . .